JAKE BLACK

By A. J. Butcher

JAKE BLACK

a Spy High novel

A. J. Butcher

www.atombooks.co.uk

A paperback original from *Atom* Books

First published in Great Britain by Atom 2005

Copyright © 2005 by Atom Books

Based on concepts devised by Ben Sharpe
Story by A. J. Butcher

The right of A. J. Butcher to be identified as author of this Work has been asserted by him in accordance with the Copyright, Designs and Patents Act 1988.

A CIP catalogue record for this book is available from the British Library.

ISBN 1 904233 38 4

Typeset in Cochin by M Rules
Printed and bound in Great Britain
by Bookmarque Ltd, Croydon, Surrey

Atom
An imprint of
Time Warner Book Group UK
Brettenham House
Lancaster Place
London WC2E 7EN

www.twbg.co.uk

For the Parkstone Grammar School
English Department 1997–2003: Gill,
Phil, Theresa, Julie and Helen

PROLOGUE

In the Domes it was never dark. The artificial suns that hovered beneath the mighty glasteel arches were never allowed to set. They existed only to provide the optimum amount of light to quicken the growth of crops, just as the sole purpose of the Domes themselves was to safeguard and sustain the prime agricultural land of the American Midwest. Each one, soaring higher than a cathedral, enclosing within it hundreds of acres of golden wheat like treasure, a shining symbol of man's ability to bring order to his world. In the Domes the earth was never scorched, never frozen. Storms never raged; tornadoes never ravaged. In the Domes all was controlled, predictable. And the people who lived under their sheltering curves, the Domer farmers, were grateful for that.

At least, most of them were.

'Are you sure this is a good idea?' The tone of eight-year-old Lonny's voice suggested he felt not, a suspicion reinforced by the anxiety in his pale blue eyes. But then, everything about Lonny was pale. 'Jake, are you *sure*?'

'Lonny's got a point, Jake.' Ford scratched his head, a sure sign of nervousness. His hair grew like the wheat and matched the colour, too. 'There's still time if we decide to . . . you know . . .'

Jamie watched the fourth and final member of the little group intently and said nothing. She wasn't going to be the one to back out.

The black-haired boy gave no immediate indication that he'd heard his friends. His attention instead seemed to remain fixed on the old, rusting wheelless truck that had pulled up to the Border Zone checkpoint. Then, with a suddenness that made them start, he snapped his head round and was crouching with them again behind the crates.

'Okay,' he said, urgent and excited. 'It's now or never. Am I sure this is a good idea, Lonny?' Locking on to the pale boy with dark, compelling eyes. 'It's something we're not supposed to do, isn't it? We're supposed to be good little boys and girls and never leave the Dome, aren't we? Well sucks to that. This is a *very* good idea. And Ford – there's still time if we decide to what? Creep back home again with our tails between our legs? I didn't come all this way just to gawp at the Border Zone for an hour. Who would?' He glanced with distaste at the wretched shanty town that huddled close to the wall of the Dome itself. 'We want out, don't we? Watch says it's night outside, real night, black skies and stars, and that's something I *do* want to see. Thought you did too. Jamie?' He finally turned to her. Always save the best till last.

'I'm with you, Jake,' the girl said. 'You can rely on me.'

He smiled, irresistibly. He'd known that already. She might be a bit freckly at the moment, and they might both still have a couple of years to go before they even reached double figures, but when they were old enough, Jake was going to marry Jamie.

First things first, though. 'What about you two?' Difficult to keep the contempt for cowards from his voice.

'I guess so,' offered Lonny. 'But Jake, what if we're seen?'

'We won't be. Not if we're quick.'

'Lonny's got a point, Jake,' said Ford, scratching furiously. 'The guards . . . you know . . .'

'Keep that up you'll get a splinter,' Jake warned. Jamie grinned. 'The guards are nothing. They wouldn't notice if a terrorist attack brought the Dome down around their ears. Besides' – a glance confirmed it – 'they're checking the guy's transit papers. Now are we going or not?'

Three nods, but only one with commitment. Good enough.

'Then let's *do* it.'

They darted across the roadway from the crates to the truck. Jake was in the lead, naturally. He was enjoying it, Jamie saw, was moving with stealthy slickness like he was some kind of secret agent or something. But he wasn't. He was a farmer's child like the rest of them, and in time they'd grow up to have farmer's children of their own. Jamie was looking forward to it. Little Jamies. Little Jakes.

And he was right about the guards, of course. Bored

with their station, or incompetent, or both. Oblivious to a quartet of children scrambling on to the back of a battered wheelless truck, smuggling themselves under tarpaulin sheets that by rights belonged to the previous century, not 2056. Someone was holding her hand and squeezing it reassuringly. Jake. Someone else was whimpering. Lonny. 'Keep quiet,' Jake hissed. 'It won't be for long.'

It wasn't. They heard the slamming door as the driver rejoined his vehicle, the whoosh of the magnetic motor charging. They felt the forward motion, slow and steady. An essential part of Jake's plan. Speeds on the transitway, the road that cut through the Border Zones on both sides of the Dome, were strictly controlled. The trucker's unexpected passengers would be bailing out way before he accelerated.

Jake peeped from beneath the tarpaulin. The Dome, like some gigantic sunken light-bulb, was already to their rear. They'd passed through the final checkpoint unchallenged. Dark and empty land stretched away into incalculable distances. The sight of it made him tremble. He didn't dare yet look up.

'Jump!' he ordered the others. 'This is it. Jump!'

He didn't wait for them. Let them keep up if they could. This was something Jake had to do and he had to do it now. Heart hammering like a drumroll, he threw off the tarpaulin and leapt from the truck. He was aware of Jamie beside him, of falling through a blackness as through ink, and then the luminous strip of the transitway rising to meet him. He rolled with the impact, the surface hard and unyielding. If there was pain, Jake didn't feel it. As he scrambled again to his feet, he felt only awe.

Above him, unfettered by the Dome, infinite and illimitable, the night sky gaped in all its ebon glory.

Jake stared into the darkness of its depths as if entranced. 'We made it,' he breathed. 'We're here.'

'Jake.' Jamie was tugging at his sleeve.

'Can you see it, Jamie? No walls. No barriers. Nothing to stand in your way.'

'*Jake.*'

It was Lonny and Ford. They'd followed his lead from the wheelless but they were still on their knees on the transitway. Not injured. Terrified. Lonny was physically shaking and Ford had forsaken his scratching regime in favour of employing both hands to cover his head, as if he anticipated being struck from above at any moment. They averted their eyes from the vastness of the sky like savages too fearful to look upon their god.

'It's too big,' Lonny moaned. 'It's too dark.' He clung to the luminous road as if he was on the brink of a precipice and the transitway was the only thing that kept him from falling.

'Lonny's got a . . . he's right,' Ford wailed.

They were only children after all, and the Dome had kept them safe.

'We've got to go back.' Lonny shook his head miserably. 'This was a stupid idea and we can't stay here. We've got to go back.'

Jake glared the way they'd come. They were only just beyond the lights of the Dome as it was, its confining arch. Did everyone hate their home as much as he did?

'Not yet, Lonny,' he responded. 'Not me. I'm going on.'

'On *where*?' Ford demanded incredulously.

'Out there.' Jake pointed into the night, towards invisible destinations.

'You can't go out there.' Lonny seemed genuinely concerned. 'Jake, don't. You don't know what's out there. It's so dark. What if you get lost?'

'Are you coming?' Jake addressed the question only to Jamie. 'Come with me. Just a little way.'

She hung her head. 'I can't. I'm like the others, Jake. I'm scared.'

'But I'll look after you. You know that. I won't let anything bad happen.' He was bewildered that she didn't appear to believe him. 'Jamie?'

'I only want to go home, Jake. I'm sorry. This is all too much. It's too much.'

Jake smiled bitterly. 'You said you were with me. You said I could rely on you.'

'Stay with me,' Jamie invited. 'Jake, stay here with us. Come back with us.'

'Not yet.' He gazed upwards. He gazed outwards. The blackness, total and absolute, was tempting him on. 'I won't be long. Will you wait for me? Can you do that? Wait here until I get back? I just want to . . .' He indicated the sprawling dark. 'I just want to know what it's like.'

'We're not supposed to be outside the Dome,' Lonny was whimpering. 'The Dome protects us from the dark.'

'We'll wait,' said Jamie.

Jake nodded. His eyes shone. And then he was turning from her and stepping from the road and plunging determinedly, purposefully into the void. Perhaps he called her name. Perhaps he waved. But in seconds no sight or sound of Jake Daly remained. He was swallowed by silence, drowned by the dark.

'Why does he always do these things?' complained Lonny. 'What's he trying to prove?'

'Jamie,' added Ford, 'what if Jake *never* comes back?'

But the girl did not reply.

Jake knew how empathy was traditionally used as a teaching tool, putting yourself in someone else's shoes in order to understand more sensitively their point of view. Putting yourself in someone else's body, however, in someone else's mind, that was taking the technique a whole stage further. Spy High's virtual reality psychological training programs were cutting-edge even for 2066.

He was standing on a Los Angeles sidewalk – or rather, the terrorist whose form he was sharing was. And then again, was it right to label the man a terrorist yet? So far he hadn't committed an atrocity. Was it more accurate to think of him as a *potential* terrorist? Jake supposed that in the end such nice distinctions didn't really matter. A fox was a fox before and after it slaughtered the farmer's chickens, and even if this guy in the long coat hadn't thus far killed anyone, he was planning to do so very soon. Within minutes. His palms were moist with the prospect.

It was a hot day but the man kept his coat buttoned to

the neck. He was perspiring freely and obviously considered deodorant to be an affectation of the decadent imperialistic West. But it wasn't the physical elements of the program that made Jake most uncomfortable, it was being so close to a mind as sick and twisted as this one.

The hatred was almost overwhelming, like a virulent disease, a contagion without a cure. Jake felt the man's facial muscles contract into a smile as he acknowledged the passers-by, the businessmen, the women shopping, parents with children. Yet simultaneously the terrorist could scarcely restrain his loathing, his contempt for those same pedestrians. And not just the hatred. There was fear too, paranoia. Every man, woman and child in the city was his enemy, would destroy him if they could, was plotting against him and against his beliefs. He'd been told this by those wiser than himself, had been told it so many times that it had become an irrefutable truth. The terrorist was isolated, alone among his enemies, and he had to get *them* before they could get *him*.

And the third thing, as the man strode towards the entrance to the subway. He *was* alone. He was one. And one was a very small number. One didn't matter. One was irrelevant. One person. One life. Only the cause mattered, the cause that was beyond the individual and therefore immortal and glorious. To serve that cause, even humbly, even for the briefest of moments, was to partake of that immortality and glory and to be redeemed. So, in a way, there *was* a one that mattered.

One sacrifice.

With a final glance at the world above, the man descended into the subway station.

Jake couldn't be sure whether the racing heart belonged to him or to his host. He wanted to hijack the terrorist's voice, to shout out and warn the crowds cramming through the securistiles to run, to flee, to get out while they could, there was a monster among them disguised as a man. The program didn't permit it. He could only watch, learn and suffer.

'Excuse me, sir.' A vigilant security guard. 'If you could just step over here for a moment, please.' Away from the stream of people. These people would now live. Those five minutes behind them would now not.

'I have a ticket.' Terrorists never went in for minor misdemeanours. 'It is a valid ticket, no?'

'Could you just open your coat for me, sir?' A hot day and the garment buttoned to the neck. 'All the way down for me, please, sir.' The terrorist grinning, strong in his mission, strong in the cause. Jake looked at the guard. A family man, he guessed. Wife, kids and dog at home. Suspecting this guy was packing something, carrying a weapon, laced with explosives. It had happened before. Confronting him. Risking his own life to maybe save others. You probably passed a hero in the street every day. Or a *potential* hero. 'Could you open your coat for me, please, sir?'

'Of course.' The terrorist obeyed. No guns. No beltloads of bombs. The security guard's relief was almost palpable. He frisked the man anyway, just to be on the safe side. 'If I had known I would be treated to this, I would ride the subway more often.'

'Can't be too cautious these days, sir. The terrorist threat. You know how things are.'

'I do indeed, my friend.'

And free to resume his journey. And laughing, exultant as he allowed the throng to bear him to the platform. Any platform. Any train. The immolation of one was as laudable as another. And it was imminent. The time of his sacrifice was near. The guard had been a fool. The means of death were not visible about his person. They were *inside* him. Bio-explosives, mingling with his blood, coursing thickly through his veins. Awaiting detonation.

The train doors closed. The carriage was packed. That was good.

Someone was reading a book they'd never finish. Two lovers making plans that would never come to pass. A man on a mobile conducting a conversation that would never be concluded. The nature of terrorism was to disrupt continuity. A victim was someone who saw the beginning of their day but not the end.

The train eased into the tunnel. It gathered pace.

And something else, Jake thought bleakly. The ruthless fanaticism. The suicidal resolution of the committed terrorist. He was in the mind of a man who would not be stopped, who was beyond reason or persuasion or the appeal of humanity.

Who was drawing from a pocket in his coat a vial of clear liquid.

'What are you drinking, mister?' said the boy in the seat next to him. 'Is it medicine?'

'Joey!' scolded his mother, and apologised.

'It doesn't matter,' said the terrorist, swigging the liquid down. 'Nothing matters now.' A weird note of triumph in his voice that made the woman clasp her son to her. 'But it was not medicine, boy. It was detonator fluid. My moment of sacrifice is upon me and you shall all die.'

The last sound Jake heard was the woman screaming.

It might have been ten years since he led his friends on their great escape from the Dome, but the teenager who now strode frowningly through the corridors of Spy High was still clearly recognisable as that same Jake Daly. The body had filled out, and impressively, given the glances it was earning from the female students Jake passed, but the hair was as black and wild as ever, as if it had only been combed on birthdays and Thanksgiving during the preceding decade, and the eyes remained dark and magnetic. There was still the sense of rage repressed, of a restless anger with the way things were and a willingness to do something about it.

'Hey, Daly, watch where you're going!' From a second-year student who Jake's self-absorbed progress had inadvertently almost knocked flying. He didn't pause. 'These graduate types, they think they own the place.'

Jake had more important things on his mind than the niceties of so-called civilised social interaction. He was chilled to the bone, despite the perfectly regulated temperature here below ground. The VR. The subway terrorist. He'd showered after exiting the program for maybe twenty minutes, trying to scour the memory of what he'd witnessed from him as if it was dirt, but it still clung. He'd never been so glad to clamber out of his cyber-cradle and get back to normal.

If Spy High could ever be called normal.

What other educational establishment could boast the kind of underground accommodation through which Jake marched now, let alone the holo-gym, the Intelligence Gathering Centre, the virtual reality chamber and all the other scientific marvels that occupied these lower levels? What other school provided study elevators for their students, rooms that resembled the former, with books and desks, but which functioned as the latter, connecting what was allowed to be seen from the surface with what had to remain hidden? Jake, dressed now in a uniform that would not have been out of place in any conservative academic institution – apart from the fact that it was bullet-proof and that the shirt's sleeve buttons could fire laser bolts – ascended. What other school populated the corridors of its gothic building and the playing fields of its ample grounds with holograms, in order to maintain the illusion that the curriculum followed here was a conventional one and most certainly did not include spycraft, escapology, Ethics in Espionage and the disablement of weapons of mass destruction? Only Spy High, as its students called it. Only the Deveraux College, as everyone else did.

And one final *what other*, as Jake made his way to the topmost floor, to the level wholly occupied by the rooms of Jonathan Deveraux, founder of the college that bore his name. What other school had for its headmaster a one-time reclusive billionaire who had actually died years ago but whose brain had been downloaded on to disk and was now stored on computer as software?

A rhetorical question. There was only one such place.

And for the last nearly three years, Jake had been part of it.

'You wanted to see me, sir?' He stood among a gleaming ensemble of sensors and circuitry, the founder's rooms a control centre operated from within the technology itself. A dozen screens suspended from the ceiling encircled him. Each one presented the image of a grey-haired man with cold, austere, almost metallic features.

'The subway terrorist program, Agent Daly,' said the twelve mouths of Jonathan Deveraux. 'I wanted to know your reaction.'

Jake's upper lip curled into a snarl. 'I had kind of an emotional reaction to it actually, sir.' He realised his fists were clenched.

Jonathan Deveraux might have seen that too, or he might not. 'You are, of course, aware that the program was based on a real atrocity that took place in Los Angeles on April the third this year.'

'I am aware of that, sir.' Through gritted teeth.

'Four hundred and sixty-three casualties,' Deveraux recorded. 'What are you thinking, Agent Daly?'

'I'm thinking if I'd met that guy, that terrorist scumbag, *before* he got to the subway, there'd only have been one casualty. Sir.'

'The problem with emotional reactions to external stimuli,' said Deveraux, 'is that they can lead to intemperate actions.' Something his superior hadn't had to worry about since his heart failed, Jake thought uncharitably. 'And an agent in the field who allows him- or herself to become governed by emotion risks behaving rashly. To discover which agents might be likeliest to succumb to their passions at potentially vital moments is one of the reasons the subway terrorist program was developed.'

'I can keep myself under control, sir,' assured Jake. 'When it matters.'

'Yet you talk about turning the terrorist into a casualty, Agent Daly,' Deveraux noted. 'You are, of course, aware of the first rule regarding the conduct of Deveraux agents in the field?'

'We don't kill,' Jake said grudgingly. 'Not unless we absolutely have no choice. Killing only makes us more like our enemies. We have to be better that that.' Words learned by rote and repeated without inflection.

'Exactly,' said Jonathan Deveraux. 'Is this a philosophy that you still find yourself able to follow, Agent Daly?'

Jake thought of the subway terrorist, what the man had been feeling, what the program had made *him* feel, the ghastly, terrible celebration of slaughter. And the Deveraux response to such fanatics? 'We don't kill. Killing only makes us more like our enemies.' Words echoing hollowly in his head.

'Agent Daly?'

'Sorry, sir, I was . . .' He frowned. 'Sir, something I think I learned from the virtual reality. This subway guy, the others like him – and they're out there, aren't they, others like him – they're not like normal criminals, not even like some of the lunatics we've fought in the past. They don't have a sense of self-preservation. They don't value their own lives so they don't care if they die. They *want* to die. How can you fight that? How can you persuade a suicide bomber that he shouldn't detonate his bomb? *Unless* you're prepared to use whatever force is necessary to stop him.'

'Even *killing* force, Agent Daly?' Jake found he couldn't meet any of the founder's twenty-four eyes. 'But Deveraux agents do not kill.'

'No, sir.' But he didn't sound convinced.

'This is *great*!' grinned Eddie Nelligan. 'The boys are back in town. Well, back in the rec room at Spy High if you want to get picky about it, but we don't care, do we, Ben, hey? Good to see you.' He punched the tall blond boy playfully in the stomach. 'Putting on a little weight though, aren't we? How you doing?'

'Better than you if you try that again, Eddie.' Ben Stanton's blue eyes narrowed.

'Still that sprightly Stanton *joie de vivre*,' Eddie observed.

'Still that never-ending Nelligan nonsense,' said Cally, draping one arm over Eddie from behind and ruffling his red hair with her other hand. 'Hush, Eddie. And can I just point out that this *isn't* a reunion exclusively for the male members of Bond Team.'

'Just as well,' put in Bex Deveraux, standing close by with Lori. 'Otherwise there'd be no chance of a decent conversation.'

'I was kind of hoping for an indecent one,' Eddie quipped. He squinted towards Lori and Bex, the first girl willowy and blonde, a front-page model come to life, the second liberally pierced and sporting hair that was as purple as Caesar's robe. 'Lo, Bex, sorry, but could you just kind of separate a bit? It's getting so hard to tell the two of you apart.'

Cally shook her dreadlocked head. 'Has anybody ever told you you're an idiot, Eddie?'

'Everybody but my shrink, and he's on long-term sick leave.'

'But it *is* good to be together again,' said Lori, 'even if Mr Deveraux hasn't told us why we're here.'

'Yeah.' Eddie refused to stay quiet. 'These days the only times we get the summons are when somebody's died.' A not altogether pleasant thought occurred to him. 'Where's Jake?'

They were taken to the screening room, where Jonathan Deveraux's head emerged from the holo-wall to greet them. Eddie half wanted to make jokes about popcorn and R-rated movies, but the mood was suddenly tense, anxious. Not that Mr Deveraux was ever a fun guy. Eddie glanced across to a grim-faced Bex. If his own father had been reduced to a computer program and now ran a worldwide espionage organisation, Eddie reckoned he might look like that as well. But Bex wasn't the issue right now. Whatever kind of feature they were to be shown, it concerned Jake.

The former members of Bond Team took their seats.

'You're wondering why Agent Daly is not with you,' Deveraux said. 'This is why.'

Footage of city rooftops flickered before them, rooftops as seen from high in the sky and gazing directly down, reduced to tiny flat squares.

'This film was taken by one of our surveillance

satellites monitoring a routine locate-and-capture mission three days ago,' Deveraux informed them.

And two days ago they'd been ordered to report to Spy High. Lori felt her heart sinking. Rooftops. The absence of Jake. It couldn't be, could it?

Jerkily, the camera moved into close-up. There were two figures hurtling across the buildings, leaping from roof to roof. One was chasing down the other. The man in the lead, swarthy, almost simian, pausing only occasionally, and then only to fire his shock blaster at his pursuer, Lori did not recognise. The pursuer himself, black-haired and evading his quarry's shots with disdainful ease before responding from the wrist with sleepshot, the boy her own age, she knew immediately even from above. Lori supposed she ought to. She'd dated Jake for months.

'What's happening? Sir?' She couldn't afford to wait for the final reel, the hero's shocking and moving death. This was real life. 'Jake doesn't . . . he isn't . . .'

'Agent Daly is alive, Agent Angel,' supplied Deveraux, but there was no emotion in his voice.

'Jake's got 'im. Look!' Eddie drew her back to the screen.

He was ahead of the game. Jake had *nearly* caught his prey. The fleeing man had launched himself through space again, and maybe once too often this time. He scarcely gained the neighbouring roof. He floundered, fell, clawed for the ledge. His fingers found it though his blaster shattered on the concrete dozens of metres below. He was dangling helplessly and Jake was leaping over his head, landing safely on the roof. Jake was doing his job. All that was left was for him to haul the Bad Guy up and take him into custody. A routine locate-and-capture mission, just as Mr Deveraux had said.

So why wasn't he doing it? Why was he simply standing there, feet apart, hands on hips, standing there tauntingly above the panicking crim?

Who seemed to be begging, who seemed to be pleading with Jake.

'Clearly, our surveillance satellites cannot record sound as well as vision,' said Deveraux, 'but our lip-reading experts have done their best to give this man voice.'

'Help me. You've got to help me up.' The room was filled with the tones of somebody who seemed more in danger of a cup of tea than a fatal plunge to the street. 'I can't hold on.' Graphic evidence of that as one hand came loose. 'Help me up. You can't just let me fall.'

And then Jake was crouching down and leaning forward. He was tilting his face to one side almost confidentially, bringing it close to the desperate crim. The lip-reader didn't believe in changing his voice for this new role. Jake sounded identical to the Bad Guy. 'If I pull you up, what are you going to do? Employ a fancy lawyer. Get off on a technicality. Time off for good behaviour. Out on the streets again and back to your old ways, ruining lives, destroying lives. I've seen it before. Too many times.'

'Not me.' The crim again. 'I promise. Please. I can't . . . then he cries out a bit' – the lip-reader intruding – 'and then it's back to . . . I can't hold on. Help me. I'll change.' The lip-reader paused. 'Then Agent Daly says, Scum like you never change. But I've changed. The system doesn't work. It's too soft. And guess what, and you're the first to know, I'm going to do something about it. See you around, scumbag.'

'See you around, scumbag?' Eddie echoed approvingly. 'How Dirty Harry is that?'

'But what's he doing?' Lori was dismayed.

Jake was getting to his feet. He was turning his back on the anguished crim. He was walking away.

'No. Jake, you can't . . .' Dismay turning to horror.

'Daly,' Ben muttered. 'I don't believe it.'

'And then there's a scream,' said the lip-reader.

Which didn't surprise any of Bond Team. Screaming was what you tended to do when your fingers lost their grip on the ledge of a building and you plummeted twenty storeys to your death. Lori could have done without the surveillance satellite's close-up of *that*.

'He let him fall.' Bex seemed more puzzled than anything. 'Jake let the guy fall.'

'He let the guy *die*,' said Cally.

'That's why you have been brought together again, Bond Team,' said Jonathan Deveraux. The film came to an end. Everybody had seen more than enough. 'The five of you know Agent Daly better than anyone else. It is only appropriate that you should do what has to be done.'

'Uh,' ventured Eddie, 'what has to be done?'

'Agent Daly has broken the first rule for all Deveraux operatives. He has caused a death when he could and should have saved a life. He has demonstrated that he is no longer fit to carry out his duties as a secret agent. He can no longer belong to this organisation.'

'Oh, no.' Lori knew what that meant.

'There is then the danger that he might compromise our work by making it public. Thus, Agent Daly must be mind-wiped, all trace of his existence with us eradicated from his memory. He must be returned to his former life.'

'Is there no other way, sir?' Lori implored.

'There is not, Agent Angel,' said Deveraux.

'But sir,' asked Ben, 'I don't quite understand. What do you need us for?'

'Our first attempt to detain him was resisted, Agent Stanton,' the founder admitted. 'Agent Daly is now on the run. Your task is therefore very simple. You must find your erstwhile partner, apprehend him, and bring him back to Deveraux for mind-wiping. And you will leave immediately.'

ONE

IGC DATA FILE STX 3073
CLASSIFICATION: TERRORISM

The security services are congratulating themselves this morning after striking what one
source described as 'a significant blow' in the
ongoing war against terror. Pre-dawn raids
across several cities on the West Coast have led
to a number of arrests of known terrorist sus-
pects. Though it has yet to be officially
confirmed, rumoured to be among those appre-
hended is Null, allegedly one of the most
trusted lieutenants of Sicarius, the leader of
the Bringers of the Night.

It is believed that Null was heading a cell of
the notorious terrorist group and in the advanced
stages of planning an attack on the power supply
of Solar City. Prompt action by the authorities
seems to have averted this possibility, though

Solar City itself has been placed on the highest level of alertness.

The people of the Free World are increasingly familiar with the Bringers of the Night. The group may be a recent addition to the ranks of the enemies of democracy, but it has already claimed responsibility for a number of outrages, including the Los Angeles subway atrocity earlier this year. Its leader, Sicarius, though rarely filmed or photographed, has earned a reputation as one of the most ruthless and fanatical terrorists at liberty today, and is the subject of a worldwide manhunt.

Sicarius may so far have eluded justice, but it seems this morning that many of his followers have not been so fortunate.

FILELINK: TERRORISM
SUB-SECTION: THE BRINGERS OF THE NIGHT
IGC DATA FILE STX 2950
SOURCE: *TODAY WITH TRACY*

'Perhaps you could elaborate further, Professor. I'm sure most people in our audience consider one terrorist to be very much like another.'

'Of course, Tracy. But research has shown that there are distinctions to be made. Those extremists whom we might collectively define as terrorists can usefully be divided into two groups. We might call them the *practical* terrorist and the *apocalyptic* terrorist. Now the practical terrorist lives pretty much in the world as we know it. He – or she – may be prepared to kill for their cause, and possibly even to die for it, but their aims are essentially political, their ends theoretically achievable. Groups that fight for their own region's independence from a larger country, for example, like the organisation Albion that demands British withdrawal from Europa. That could happen. It's possible. Their tactics are reprehensible, obviously, but the changes to society that the practical terrorist seeks to effect are at least feasible.

'The apocalyptic terrorist, on the other hand, has his – or her – eyes fixed on the impossible, the absolute. For the apocalyptic terrorist, this world is only a stepping stone to the next. His goals are so extreme that they can never be fulfilled. He talks only in terms of Heaven and Hell, no compromise, and he dreams of death. His attitude and his values are utterly incompatible with those of what we would consider to be a free society.

'The practical terrorist is a threat, but not an unreasonable one. We can negotiate with him. But the apocalyptic terrorist is beyond our reach, perhaps beyond our understanding. No deals can be done with him. He's out there, coming for us, and nothing can stop him.'

'Well, that's rather a chilling picture you've painted there, Professor. And I assume that the Bringers of the Night belong in the apocalyptic category.'

'That's right, Tracy. Their very name suggests it. Their fixation with night, with the fundamental opposites that underpin everything. Night and day. Black and white. Death and life. Extremes. Absolutes. And they are the *Bringers* of the Night. They are activists. They intend to bestow their truth upon us. The apocalyptic terrorist is a man of unshakeable certainties, a man who never questions. Why not? Because he already knows the answers.'

'We're running out of time, Professor - but don't worry, folks, I'm only talking about the show - so if we could perhaps turn our attention briefly to Sicarius himself.'

'Yes, well, the problem with Sicarius is that so few people claim to have seen him. Nobody knows very much about him. It's all part of the mystery, the aura, the legend. But here's a picture of him. I just want to talk about what this image tells me. A Caucasian male, yes, forty or so, not young but not old, physically strong and perhaps at the peak of his intellectual life. The hair, lustrous and black and flowing, as if his face is framed in night. High cheekbones, always impressive, regal, even. But the eyes, Tracy, look at the eyes. Black, too, so recolourised. He's done it for effect. Sicarius *is* the night. That's the way he wants us to think. And his expression, Tracy.

Arrogant. Contemptuous. Dismissive. Calculated to strike fear into the hearts of his enemies.'

'Not somebody you want to be sat next to at a dinner party then, Professor. Well, thank you very much for your insights but there we're going to have to leave it. Professor Carlton Huxley, ladies and gentlemen. And thank *you* at home for watching. And please, don't be frightened when you turn off the light tonight. Terrorism is a frightening subject, I know, but remember we have the wonderful men and women of our security services doing everything they can to protect us from the likes of Sicarius and the Bringers of the Night. They'll keep us safe as we sleep in our beds . . . I hope.'

They were coming for him. It was inevitable. They were coming for him and he needed to be ready.

From one of the few windows with glass still remaining in it Jake watched the sun going down. Shadows lengthened, advancing darkness reaching out to seize him. There was no point in running. They'd track him down in time. They'd find him. Best to face them here, in these crumbling tenement buildings long abandoned by residents who'd moved to the brighter prospects of the twenty-first century. *Here* was a good choice. No one to get in their way, no innocent bystanders to get hurt when the fighting started.

Because he'd have to fight them. Surrender was not an option.

Jake wondered how it would be. He'd been matched

against his partners during their training, of course he had. Martial arts. Pswords. Shoot-outs. In VR. On the Gun Run. In the gym. SkyBike pursuits across half of Massachusetts. But that had been training, and victory or defeat had mattered only to one's pride. It was different now. It was real. Futures depended on the outcome.

Could he take them? Individually, Jake thought so. Eddie, Cally, Bex, for sure. Lori, hmm. Ben? If the situation wasn't so serious, it might be fun finding out. But what if they came at him together, as a team? He'd soon know.

Jake drew back from the window. He prowled through the empty, crumbling rooms, his dark clothes rendering him almost invisible. Sleepshot wristbands on. Lenses in. Shock blaster set to Stun. He didn't want to hurt his friends unnecessarily. He hoped the same was true in reverse.

What did they think of him now anyway, his one-time team-mates? Jake smiled thinly. He'd soon know that, too.

In the end they didn't have to look too hard.

Like all Spy High personnel, Jake's unique biosignature was stored in the Deveraux databanks. In an age of radical facial reconstruction, this was seen as a vital defence against impersonation. Every ingredient of an agent's inner physical being, the characteristic electrical activity of his brain, the individual intricacies of his nervous system, the particular note and tenor of his heartbeat, everything was charted and recorded. For the former Bond Team's present purposes, that information could be used by a surveillance satellite equipped with biotracking capability to locate a given subject. The technology as yet did not provide pinpoint precision, but it could narrow a search to a specific area.

Then it was down to human pursuers.

'Typical Daly'd be hiding out somewhere like this,' Ben sniffed as their SkyBikes swooped low over the tenement roofs. 'I bet he feels right at home.'

'You're not enjoying this, are you, Ben?' Cally, alongside him, seemed a little concerned. 'I wouldn't like to think you were having a good time over this. I know the history between you and Jake hasn't all been peace treaties and positive cooperation, but even so, having to bring him in like some kind of crim when by rights he's one of us, I don't—'

'Don't *worry*, Cal,' said Ben. 'I'm *not* enjoying this. It's the opposite. Because you said it yourself. Daly was a Bond Teamer too, and what he's done reflects badly on all of us. Let's land. Down there.'

The SkyBikes descended to a street whose last lighting had long ago been extinguished. It seemed the teenagers were at the bottom of a dark canyon.

'Activate your bikes' immobilisers,' Ben instructed.

'Yes, *sir*.' Bex saluted ironically. 'And here was me thinking Lori was group leader.'

Lori said nothing, just gazed up at the unwelcoming façades of the surrounding slums. Behind one of them, Jake was waiting.

'Just as well these babies don't have hubcaps,' Eddie observed. 'If they did, in this neighbourhood they wouldn't have them for long.'

'Eddie, button it,' Ben said tersely. 'Everyone, ch —'

'Check your equipment,' Bex anticipated. 'Am I getting good at this or what?'

Each Bond Teamer wore a chameleon suit, a hooded black garment that was woven with millions of nanochips. Once activated, the chips assimilated and replicated the wearer's immediate environment, effectively rendering him or her invisible. Good for creeping up on ex-team-mates who'd crossed a line. Shock blasters in shoulder holsters. Sleepshot wristbands in place. Radar visors fixed. 'I guess that's equipment checked,' said Eddie. 'Kind of a nervy moment though, isn't it? Do you reckon there's a public convenience around here anywhere?'

'No games. No grandstanding.' Ben's eyes behind his visor were cold. 'None of us wants to do this but we don't have a choice. Mr Deveraux's orders. Jake has to be subdued so we do it quickly and efficiently and professionally. If it helps, try not to think that the target *is* Jake.'

'The target,' muttered Bex. '*Nice* and personal.'

'We'll use one-for-all tactics. I'll go in first, flush Jake out towards the rest of you, then if I haven't already put him down, you can. Okay?'

'No, Ben.' With a sigh, Lori withdrew her attention from the buildings and redirected it to her partners.

'No?'

'Get used to it, Ben,' Eddie remarked. 'That's all girls ever say to me, too.'

'One-for-all, yes, but I think in this instance you might not be the best person to take point.'

'What are you talking about, Lo?' Ben objected.

'I'll do it. I'll go in. Maybe Jake'll listen to me' – for old times' sake, she thought – 'and we can avoid violence.'

'Don't bet on it, Lori,' scoffed Ben. 'Besides—'

'There isn't a besides.' Lori was adamant. 'I don't want to pull rank on anyone but what Bex mentioned earlier, I *was* group leader of Bond Team when we graduated. I outrank everyone here because of it, and in the field it's not a democracy. *I'll* go in. All right, Ben?'

'Whatever you say, Lo.' As gracefully as he could manage. But he was thinking, you never used to be this strong-willed when you were going out with me.

'All right. Track me with your belt-tracers.' She sighed again. 'Let's get this done.'

Lori Angel vanished.

She stole through the vacant apartments like a ghost. Obviously, with her chameleon suit activated, Jake wouldn't be able to see her, and after three years of Spy High stealth and infiltration training, he didn't stand much chance of hearing her, either. The same was less true in reverse. With the aural amplifiers in her hood, she could hear not only the proverbial pin drop but the breeze through a broken pane of glass several rooms away, the scuttle of a spider, its spindly legs like the hoofs of a rhinoceros.

A lonely footfall from the storey above her.

Lori turned the amplifiers down, signalled to her team-mates that she'd located their target. It had to be Jake. She wanted it to be Jake.

And it was. She glided up stairs as if she was floating. He was there by the window of a room, keeping watch, concentration intense but misdirected. His hiding-place had already been breached.

She could shoot him from here.

But Lori couldn't do that, not shoot him in the back, not even with an essentially harmless sleepshot shell. Not Jake. She had to get closer. She'd been closer to him once, and the heartbeat that the chameleon suit now silenced had quickened when he was near. It was doing so again, but for different reasons.

Lori stalked Jake.

His attention was fixed on the night outside. He looked mournful, lost. His strength had always masked a melancholy. She advanced towards him, was almost on him. She would reach out, touch his shoulder with cobweb lightness, and as he turned she would use her sleepshot and for Jake it would all be over. Sadly, with regret, she was stretching out her hand —

'Sorry, Lo.' Jake swivelling, a blur. 'You want to creep up on somebody like that' – seizing her arm, yanking, throwing her, the world turned upside down – 'pick a guy who's not wearing spectrolenses.' She slammed to the floor and gasped. 'Chameleon suit doesn't work on me.'

'So tell me what will.' Lori pressed the belt stud to deactivate the suit, pulled her hood back, her blonde hair cascading free. 'Talk to me, Jake.'

'About what?' He sounded to Lori almost rueful. 'What I've got to say you won't want to hear.'

'You let that man die, Jake. Why?'

'You know why, Lori.' Bitterly. 'You know how I feel

about Deveraux's methods. They're soft. They're useless. And I know you think otherwise. It pretty much split us up, remember? Well now I'm doing something about it. I don't expect you to understand.'

Lori was on her feet again. She felt maddened, frustrated. 'But I *want* to understand.'

'No time, babe. If you're here then Stanton and the others are here too.' Jake tensed. 'You think you can take me, Lo?'

Couldn't be distracted by old times now. Deploy sleepshot and have done. Lori raised her wrist and fired. Slow motion to Jake. He barrelled into her (not the kind of close physical contact they'd once enjoyed). She shifted her weight, threw Jake over her hip. He landed on his back, was kicking out even as she prepared to fire sleepshot a second time. His boot knocked her arm aside. Could have followed up with a crippling ram into her stomach. Chose instead to sweep her legs from under her. Lori's turn to go down. She rolled instinctively, aware that Jake too was armed. She coiled like a spring, ready to renew her own attack.

But her opponent was already at the door. Jake, fleeing. Afraid she'd defeat him or that he might hurt her? No choice but to shoot again now, and Lori's aim was 99.9 per cent perfect. The 0.1 per cent had the sleepshot pellets chipping the door frame. Jake's disappearing back was intact.

Why didn't that dismay her?

'He's coming your way, guys.' Lori spoke into her communicator. If there'd been a source of water around, she'd have been tempted to wash her hands.

On the roof, Ben received his team-mate's warning with a mixture of disdain and self-satisfaction. That was what they got for sending Lori to do what had clearly been *his* job.

'And he's wearing spectrolenses. Ixnay the cham suits.'

Sure. Fine. Nowhere to hide. Just the way he liked it.

'No chances, guys.' Ben led the way in training their wristbands on the door to the stairwell. Soon as Daly burst through there, it was slumber city.

The door promptly exploded.

Shards of wood speared at the Bond Teamers, scattering them, breaking their focus. Jake took full advantage.

He threw himself low through the now gaping doorway, his shock blaster, reset from Materials to Stun, blazing. Eddie was slower with his feet than he was with his mouth. A blast caught him square on and spun him to the floor. Jake was forward-rolling beneath Cally and Ben's crossfire, bounding up again to smash into an immobile Bex, grasped her, twisted her round, using her as a shield.

Cally paused, confronted by her struggling team-mate. Pausing in the middle of a battle wasn't wise. Jake's blaster notched up a second direct hit.

'Daly, that's enough!' Ben had not paused. He'd pounded across the rooftop and now battered into Jake, heedless of Bex. All three combatants crashed to the concrete, Bex coming off worst, temporarily concussed.

The two boys rose. Both had dropped their blasters in the fall.

'You'd have better been using Stun,' Ben advised.

Jake for a second looked hurt that even his long-time rival might have imagined otherwise. 'Only we've seen what you're capable of these days.'

'You've seen nothing, Stanton,' Jake retorted. 'You're blind.'

They circled each other warily.

'What's that supposed to mean?' said Ben. 'Is there something you're not telling us? What really happened on that rooftop, Jake?'

'Some of the same as what's going to happen on this one,' Jake said. 'I walk away.'

'Can't let you do that, Jake.'

'One-for-all tactics,' he derided. 'I mean, honestly, Ben. Did you forget I've been to Spy High too? I'm only surprised you didn't come after me yourself first off.'

'Saved the best till last.'

'You think you're the best?'

'Shall we find out?'

The swiftness and ferocity of Ben's assault would have finished most opponents almost at once, but he and Jake had both been trained by the same masters of the martial arts at Spy High, and they'd both been taught that in any form of unarmed combat, defensive skills were as necessary to ultimate victory as the ability to attack. Jake for one had learned that lesson well. He defended, he deflected, he drew the sting from a barrage of powerful blows.

'Is this it, Ben? You're slipping in your old age.' Taunt him. Goad him. Play on his vanity, the old Stanton arrogance. That was the way to beat Ben.

'Why, you —' And here it came, the intemperate lunge,

the right arm exposed, the balance tipping forward. Grab it. Throw him.

'Idiot!' Ben twisted with quicksilver speed. The lunge had been a ploy. He hadn't lost control at all. He'd second-guessed Jake's tactics and used them against him. He was behind him now, pinning Jake's arms to his sides. 'The old taunt-him, goad-him routine,' Ben derided. 'I mean honestly, Jake. Did you forget I've been to Spy High too?'

'How could I? You never shut up about it.' He couldn't break Ben's grip and the others were stirring again. Bex was almost fully recovered. He couldn't suffer the indignity of Stanton defeating him. 'But you've done well, Ben. How about a lie-down?'

Suddenly Jake thrust himself back against Ben, pushing with all his strength. The move surprised the blond boy. Too late he tried to resist it. The momentum was all with Jake. Ben staggered backwards, missed his footing, felt himself toppling. He ought really to have released his captive and used his arms to lessen the impact of his fall. Jake was relying on that being the *last* thing Ben would do. He was right. They hit the roof hard, but Ben hit it the harder.

Jake pulled himself free. He was dazed a little, but he reckoned he could still have made the leap from this rooftop to the next. He'd had a lot of practice lately. 'Jake!' But ah, here came Lori again.

She emerged from the stairwell, at once took in what had been happening. Jake was eyeing up the ledge. He was on the brink of escape. She raised her left arm. And Jake wasn't moving. The fight must have left him groggier than he appeared. She fired once. Didn't miss this time.

The sleepshot shell burrowed through Jake's clothing and sank into the skin of his chest, injecting its anaesthetic into his bloodstream. 'Lo . . .' he breathed. 'I'm . . .'

By the time he'd completed his crumple to the floor, Jake was unconscious.

One by one they were permitted to see him. The condemned man in his cell – Spy High style.

Cally.

'You helped me so much in the early days, Jake. I want to help you now. There must be something I can do. Tell me. There's got to be a way out.'

And Jake, regarding the detention chamber contemplatively, the energy bars criss-crossing the doorway, the observer cameras set into the walls like giant, unblinking eyeballs: 'Think it might be a bit late for that, Cal.'

Bex.

'I don't know how you can bear to look at me.'

'It's not so bad, Bex. You've had blue hair before.'

'Jake, you know what I mean. It's my dad's fault that this is happening to you and it *shouldn't* be happening. What if I go and see him? What if I try . . .?'

'It's not your dad's fault, Bex. He might have laid down the rules but we all knew what they were. I did what I did. Now I have to take the consequences.'

Eddie.

'There is one bonus in all this, Ed. At least I won't have to listen to your lame jokes any more.'

'Yeah, well at the risk of sounding serious for about

the first time in living memory, Jake, I keep thinking *this* is some kind of joke, you in a detention chamber waiting to be mind-wiped.'

'Yeah? Well if that's right, someone's got a sick sense of humour.'

Ben.

'Didn't expect to see you here, Stanton. What is it? Come to gloat?'

'Come to make an admission. On the rooftop the other night, you were the better man. You beat me fair and square. I underestimated you, Jake. I have a feeling I've always underestimated you.'

'Ah, you're only telling me that now because you know in a few hours' time I won't be able to remember it.'

'So I might as well carry on, then. You were a good secret agent, Daly. It's been a privilege working with you. I mean it. I . . . What's with the shaking head?'

'Past tense, Ben. *Were* a good secret agent. Looks like I'm history.'

Lori.

'It's all wrong, Jake, all of it.'

'Don't, Lo. It's not . . . You don't know. I'm not worth it.'

'You know what the worst thing is? The worst thing is that they'll take away what we had together, they'll wash it from your mind like our relationship was a stain or something. All those moments, all those memories, you'll be denied them, Jake.'

'They can try.'

'But I'll remember them, Jake. I'll remember *you*. I promise.'

❖

There was one-way glass in the viewing room. The witnesses gathered therein could watch quite comfortably events unfolding in the memory adjustment chamber on the other side, but the techs beyond could not see them. Neither would the subject.

Lori stared numbly at the innocently gleaming apparatus that would soon be put to use. Computer banks humming idly while they waited. The empty chair, its frame of steel but plushly upholstered, like a dentist's chair but for the shackles at wrist and ankle, hinting at a purpose more sinister than a little root-canal work. The helmet suspended from the ceiling, the golden helmet like a crown that only a fool would wear, the helmet with the electrodes at the temples. The mind-wiper itself.

'You mean the memory adjustment helmet,' the tech corrected one of Lori's team-mates, she didn't know who. They were all there. Except for Jake and he'd be along in a moment. 'Technically, of course, the process does not so much *remove* memories as *revise* them. Clearly, we need to eradicate from the subject's brain any recollection of the true work of the Deveraux College. A simple implantation of memory inhibitors is sufficient for that. The more complex operation is to alter for ever the subject's perception of his own past. It would be impractical to eliminate all knowledge of Deveraux or the people he met here from his mind – it could be done straightforwardly enough, but would then require a similar process to be carried out on everybody within the subject's wider acquaintance who was aware of his attendance at this school. No, what we do instead is substitute a set of artificial memories – happy ones, we want the subject to have enjoyed his time with us – for the reality. We give him a new past. And with regard to his relations with his fellow students, we adjust those, too. Former Agent Daly will remember you all, but as one remembers facts learned from an encyclopaedia. He will be allowed to retain no emotion towards any of you, no extremes. Extremes are potentially dangerous. You will be names. You will be faces. No more. Now the true genius of the adjustment technique is –'

'Does it hurt?' interjected Lori sharply. 'I don't care about the genius involved in messing with people's minds. I want to know, will Jake suffer?'

'Calm yourself, Agent Angel,' said the tech. 'The process is quite painless.'

'You want to go out, Lo?' Ben, concerned, touching her hand tenderly. 'You're obviously upset. Understandably. Why stay?'

'Because if I don't see it, Ben, I won't believe it.'

On the other side of her, Bex groaned. 'I'm seeing it and I *still* don't believe it.'

Flanked by two guards, Jake Daly entered the memory adjustment chamber. He was unbound but showed no inclination to try to escape. His back was straight and he held his head high. He bore himself not with shame, not with fear, but with pride.

'This isn't happening,' Lori muttered under her breath. 'Jake, what's going on?'

He was seeking his partners through the glass. He knew they were there. He was seeking *her*. And when his eyes instinctively locked with hers, when somehow he sensed that he'd found her and allowed himself a small, rueful smile, she found it hard to keep the tears from coming.

Jonathan Deveraux would change his mind. It'd be like in the movies, an innocent man going to the electric chair, Dead Man Walking, and the last-minute pardon from the Governor. Execution stayed. Life saved. All's well that ends well.

Last minute.

One of the guards made to take Jake's arm. He was shrugged off contemptuously. Jake knew where he had to go. He knew what had to happen. He seated himself in the chair unprotestingly, a willing sacrifice.

The shackles snapped shut.

Where was Deveraux? Surely he could see this was wrong. He was a computer program, for God's sake. Surely a computer program knew right from wrong.

The techs were telling Jake to relax. They were fluttering at the controls. The memory adjustment helmet flashed red lights like warnings. It was alive.

No reprieve. No last-gasp rescue.

Deveraux didn't care.

The helmet descended. It pressed against Jake's skull.

But he was still gazing at her, his eyes full of entreaty, begging for understanding. Then the visor flashed down like a guillotine. Lori would never see Jake's face again.

'Do something,' she urged. 'We've got to do something.' Futilely.

The mind-wiping began.

TWO

In the Domes it was never dark, which suited Jake Daly just fine. It meant he could toil in his father's fields not only from dawn to dusk but beyond. Every day he could be seen there, a lone figure in an endless expanse of wheat, working without pause, working without complaint, working without question. Every day for Jake Daly was the same, just as it was for every other Domer farmer and Domer farmer's son. He rose early, breakfasted frugally, took no interest in the news from the outside world. He tended the crops, repaired any machinery around the farm that might require it, and when his muscles and his bones ached too sorely from his endeavours for him to continue, he retired for a late meal and a welcome bed. His existence was purely physical, a series of concrete tasks to be completed. There was no time for ambition, no place for dreams. And it would be this way for Jake Daly today, tomorrow, for the rest of his life.

His parents were delighted, particularly his father.

Mr Daly hadn't wanted to send his only son to that fancy school hundreds of miles away in the first place. 'I don't know why I allowed it,' he told friends. 'That tutor fella who came to see us, Grunt or Grint or whatever he called himself, he must have been purty persuasive, is all I can say. But I shouldn't have wasted my time fretting. Jake's got too much sense to be taken in by the outside world for long. I should have known he'd come back to us sooner or later. He's a Domer born and bred. He'll make his old pa proud of him yet.'

'Why *did* you come back, Jake?' his sister Beth asked him one day after bringing him his lunch in the far field. She was nearly eleven now, a grave, thoughtful girl with hair as black and unkempt as her brother's, only longer.

'Why?' Jake frowned as if the question had not occurred to him. 'What's the matter, Beth? Do you wish I hadn't?'

'Of course not. I love it that you're here. I've missed having a big brother to stand up for me. It's just that you seemed so happy at the Deveraux College, and then after you graduated, travelling the world as a youth ambassador for the Deveraux Foundation, it all seemed so exciting, you seemed to love it so much. I only wondered . . .'

'Sometimes it takes you a while to realise what you really love, Beth, what you truly want out of life. You'll understand better when you're older.'

'Ah!' the girl laughed. 'That's what I've missed too, having a big brother to talk *down* to me. Same old Jake.'

'You think so, huh?' Jake smiled warmly. 'Thanks for

the food. Now why don't you let me get back to work and go play with your dolls or something?'

'Jake,' Beth protested, 'I'll be eleven next birthday. Playing with dolls is *so* single figures. And you're not getting rid of me *that* easily. What about your friends from school, the ones who came here? Ben. Cally. Are you still in touch with them?'

'No, I kind of lost touch with them,' mused Jake. 'I guess we didn't have much in common when it came down to it.' He gazed pensively into the distance.

'You must still want to see the Angel girl, though,' persisted Beth. 'I thought she was a real angel, didn't I, made her take me for a ride on her SkyBike. You came too if I remember rightly, big brother.'

'Did I? Can't remember.'

'Hmm.' Beth was suspicious. 'Lori. Don't tell me you've forgotten about Lori, Jake. You couldn't take your eyes off her when she was here.'

'Things change,' Jake said. 'People change. That's something else—'

'Argh!' Beth threw up her hands in manic self-defence. 'Don't say it!'

They said it together: 'You'll understand better when you're older.'

'Why so interested anyway?' Jake said. 'Nosing into other people's business is *so* single figures, little sister.'

'I don't know. Maybe because there's nothing interesting in the Dome.'

'What?'

'Can I tell you a secret, something I wouldn't dare tell Ma or Pa?' The girl looked at her brother warily. 'I'm thinking I want to be like you, Jake, when I'm older.' A momentary grin.

'Like me how?' But he knew.

'Leave the Dome. Make a life for myself outside. *See* things. *Do* things.' She closed her eyes dreamily. 'You can help me, Jake. You've seen more of the outside world than anybody in the Dome. You can *prepare* me.'

'I can't.' Jake's reply was flat and final. 'I *won't*.'

'Jake?' The girl blinked at her brother unhappily.

'Go home, Beth. Forget about leaving. Your place is here. My place is here.' His voice was emotionless. 'It always will be.'

The terrorists appeared in the doorways on either side of the street. Lori was unconcerned. She held a shock blaster in each hand. Right and left, she fired them simultaneously. The animate figures flashed green for disengaged and her score increased. She raised her arms higher. They'd be at the windows above the shopfronts next. The programmers of the Gun Run had a thing about varying the attacks not simply by location but by height as well. True to form, dark shadows over the florist's. She turned them green with a squeeze of the triggers. At least they were in the right place for a wreath.

It was all too easy. But then, Lori hadn't selected Static Mode in order to test her combat abilities. She'd activated the Gun Run for a different reason today.

'Don't tell me.' Bex was sauntering unarmed up the street behind her. 'Neat way of working off some tension.'

A terrorist on the roof had spotted her. He was preparing to fire. 'Bex, look out!' Lori got a round off first and Bex didn't have to look anywhere.

'Don't panic, Lo,' she said coolly. 'I'm not even wearing a ShockSuit. You're the one who's in for a few volts if any of the Osamas get lucky.'

Bex was right, and while the electric shocks for being struck by a terrorist blast were mild, delivered by sensors in the outwitted agent's suit in the manner of unpleasant-tasting medicine administered by a doctor, Lori had no wish to experience one due to her friend's appearance breaking her concentration. 'Program: pause,' she instructed.

'Program paused, Agent Angel,' said the street politely.

'The others have gone,' Bex reported, safe now from the intervention of animates out to kill her. 'Back to their own assigned areas of operation. Bond Team dissolved again until the next one of us breaks the rules.'

Lori winced, seemed to find something of interest in the toe of her boot. 'You interrupted my Run to tell me something I already know? You're a very caring person, Rebecca.'

'I'm glad my interpersonal skills haven't gone unnoticed,' Bex said. 'So am I right?'

'About what?' Sullenly.

'Why you're here. Why you've got Osamas lined up like sitting ducks. Releasing tension. Coping mechanism.'

'Coping with what, Bex?' Defensively.

'Come on, Lo. Don't get simple on me. Four letters. Begins with J. Used to be your partner, in more ways than one. I know you're still hurting over Jake.' Bex's tone became gentler. She might have been pierced in strange places by cold metal, but the skin beneath was warm. 'We all are. But it hit you hardest of all, didn't it?' She glanced around her. 'Seems to me shooting at hunks of steel that are trying to shoot *you* isn't going to be much help, though. Talking to a friend, on the other hand . . .'

'Maybe.' Lori looked up at Bex and smiled sheepishly. 'Do you know where I can find one?'

They strolled the Gun Run arm in arm.

'It's not only the fact that Jake's gone I'm having trouble coming to terms with,' Lori confided. 'It's what happened *before* the mind-wipe too.'

'What we saw on the film?'

'Not really. That was a shock, yeah, but I know Jake was what you might call frustrated with the Deveraux way of doing things. I just never thought he'd go that far.' Lori's expression was one of puzzlement. 'No, what really bothers me is what happened when we caught up with him, that night on the rooftop. Something's not quite right . . .'

'You didn't expect Jake just to hand himself in, did you?' said Bex. 'Not even to you, Lo.'

'No. I expected him to fight.'

'Well he did that,' Bex acknowledged. 'I was seeing double all the next day. Let's face it, he almost beat all five of us.'

'That's exactly it,' Lori said, excited. 'He almost did. You and the others were down, I was rushing on to the roof, and Jake was standing there and he could have leapt to the next building before I got off a sleepshot. I'm sure of it.'

'What do you mean, Lo?' Bex's turn to be puzzled.

'Program,' Lori called, 'resume.'

'Program resumed, Agent Angel,' said the street obediently. An animate ahead of them reading a newspaper suddenly dropped it and produced a pulse rifle instead.

'Static Mode,' Lori informed her companion. 'The Osamas can aim and fire, but they can't move to get out of the way when I do *this*.' The shot struck the animate right between the eyes. It seemed that green was becoming contagious. 'Program: pause.'

'And the meaning of that little outburst of violence was?' prompted Bex.

'Jake was like that, on the rooftop. He could have eluded my shot, he's fast enough. He could have kept running. But it was like he was on Static Mode, Bex. It was like he *wanted* me to stop him.'

'Okay,' said Bex. 'Next question: *why?*'

Lori shook her head in bafflement. 'Bex, I have no idea.'

He waited until long after the windows had switched to full black. Night might not be allowed to fall in the Domes, but research had proved that people still slept better when there was at least a semblance of darkness: every Domer home was equipped with the latest light-alterable windows. Jake lay in his bed until silence and stillness had settled on the Daly farm like layers of dust.

Then he got up.

He was soundless dressing, slinking through the

house. Past his parents' room, and maybe his pa wouldn't be quite so proud of his freshly restored son if he knew what Jake was about right now. Past his sister's, and maybe, when or if this was ever all over, maybe he should talk to Beth about the world beyond the Dome as she'd wanted. But maybe he wouldn't tell her everything.

Jake slipped outside. Once again he was turning his back on his past, but it couldn't be helped. If anybody saw him now they might have imagined him a lurker or a thief. He couldn't do much about that, either.

The arrangement had been to rendezvous in the barn.

The smell of hay greeted his nostrils as he eased the door open, narrowly, a sliver sufficient for him to edge through.

Someone had entered the barn before him. Someone was hiding in the shadows. When he registered the new arrival, the someone came forward.

'Am I glad to see you,' said Jake.

'Odd place to meet,' observed Lori, taking her seat opposite Bex anyway.

Bex surveyed the restaurant. Tables. Diners. Waiters. Meals. Probably a thousand others essentially identical in Boston alone. 'Odd?' she considered. 'Bearing in mind the last place we met was a mock-up of a street operated by computer and populated by several dozen murderous animates. You call that normal, Lo?'

'You know what I mean,' Lori said. 'We don't usually have to relocate to town just to talk.'

'You've been looking peaky lately,' said Bex. 'Thought you could benefit from a half-decent lunch inside you.'

Lori leaned forward. 'What's going on, Bex? Why aren't we in the rec room at Spy High?'

Bex leaned forward too, and her tone was suddenly serious. 'Because I've got something real important to say, Lori, and I didn't want to say it where my dad might hear.'

'I don't understand.'

'Walls have ears, Lo, you know that old saying? With the walls at Spy High I reckon it could be true. Electronic ears. Bugs, if you like, with Jonathan Deveraux, my esteemed late father, listening in twenty-four/seven.'

Lori creased her brow doubtfully. 'You're not telling me that Mr Deveraux actually spies on *us*, his own students, his own agents?' His own daughter, she thought. 'What's in that glass, Bex?'

Whatever it was – and it looked like water – Bex took a sip. 'No, I'm not telling you that. Maybe not. I've got no evidence anyway. On the other hand . . . I just didn't want to take the chance, not with what I've found out, 'cause it seems Dad's already keeping some secrets from us. So that's why I asked you here, Lo, where nothing we discuss can possibly get back to him. Not unless these menus are bugged . . .'

'Bex,' frowned Lori, 'are you going to begin making sense any time soon? What's this all about?'

'In a word? Jake.'

'*What?*'

'Are you ready to order?' asked the waiter.

Lori felt readier to physically assault him for the interruption, but such a course of action would likely prove counterproductive. She ordered the first dish off the menu, scarcely noticed what it was. Food was irrelevant. Another word with four letters was all that mattered to her now.

Jake. Bex had found out something about Jake? The waiter was out of earshot. '*Tell me,*' Lori demanded.

'Okay.' Bex retrieved from her jacket pocket a minicomp, a voice-activated computer the size of a mobile phone. 'What you said on the Gun Run, how you reckoned Jake could have made good his escape, it piqued my interest. I kind of hacked into the Deveraux mainframe . . .'

'You *kind of* hacked into the Deveraux mainframe?'

'Is there an echo in here or what? Yes, Lo, I kind of hacked in, and then I kind of downloaded that film of Jake letting the crim perform his Humpty Dumpty routine and I ran it through a few tests, including microanalysis. And I discovered something kind of interesting. Bring up File Jake-37,' Bex ordered the minicomp.

Its screen presented to the two girls the terrified face of a crim clinging to the ledge of a rooftop for dear life.

'Focus on pupil,' Bex said. 'Continuous enlargement.'

The man's eyes, already wide and staring with abject horror, bulged larger still. And then there was one. And then there was only the pupil of one, a disc of black despair. And then . . .

'I don't believe it,' gasped Lori.

'Pause enlargement,' said Bex.

The minicomp had done its work. Around the rim of the pupil, as invisible to the naked eye as it was intended to be, a sequence of numbers and letters in white. A serial code.

'The crim was an animate.' Lori struggled to comprehend the implications. 'Jake let an animate fall? Did he know? I mean . . .'

'He knew all right, and he wasn't the only one. I cross-referenced the serial code. Guess what?' Bex made the sound of a buzzer. 'Too late. Agent Angel reports for mind-wiping. The animate's one of ours. Manufactured by Deveraux in the good old USA.'

'So the whole scene was faked?'

'Absolutely. With Jake's willing participation. With Dad's. Must have been. And for our benefit. How else but with the evidence of their own eyes could Jake's former team-mates be persuaded to hunt him down and haul him back to Spy High for the mind-wipe?'

The enormity of Bex's intelligence dawned on Lori. 'But if the death of the crim was a sham . . .'

'So might the mind-wipe have been. I know,' nodded Bex. 'I told you my dad was keeping secrets. And just while you seem incapable of coherent speech, Lo – and maybe just close the mouth a little bit there, I know you've never courted the dumb blonde look, that's better – *I'll* come back to the biggie again. W.H.Y. Question mark. In capital letters.'

'Well I'm going to find out.' If there was a possibility that Jake *hadn't* been mind-wiped after all, that the entire episode had been a deception for reasons thus far unknown, Lori was determined to pursue it. 'I'm not due back on the West Coast for another couple of weeks. Think I'll take a trip out to the Domes. I hear the corn looks mighty fine this time of year. Might look up an old friend while I'm there.'

'I'm coming with you,' declared Bex.

'Bex, you don't have to . . .'

'I *do* have to.' Emphatically. 'I don't know what's going on with Jake, but my dad's responsible and that makes it my responsibility too. Unless, of course, you'd rather—'

'Two garden salads,' announced the waiter.

'Sorry, man,' said Lori. 'Better try and replant them. *We've* got to be somewhere else.'

He must have seen them while they were still some distance away, but if he had, Jake was not reacting. He kept on working.

Lori had suspected they might find him in the famous 'far field' of the Daly farm. Of course, it helped that she'd been here before, not just to Jake's home but to the Dome itself. Bex had previously visited neither, and it showed. First, as their SkyBikes had jetted above the wheat, leaving the Border Zone behind them, she'd behaved as if she was a tourist rather than a graduate secret agent, so distracted by the novelty of her surroundings that once or twice she'd nearly fallen off. Second, as she'd become accustomed to the omnipresent arch of the Dome, she'd begun to respond differently: 'Hey, Lo, can you get claustrophobia in a space thirty miles across? I'm starting to feel like a bug in a jar. Now I know why Jake had to leave.' But it was why he'd returned that troubled Lori.

More so when the girls landed their bikes in the far

field. The way he refrained from acknowledging them. The way he wielded what appeared incongruously to be an old-fashioned pickaxe, raising it over his head and bringing it down with monotonous, unvarying regularity, like a lifer condemned to hard labour, cutting a channel in the earth. He was wearing a pair of faded dungarees and, despite the vigour of his exertions, the exposed flesh of his upper body showed little sign of perspiration.

Lori and Bex approached him, Lori realising with a start that they were instinctively doing so cautiously.

'Doesn't exactly look pleased to see us, does he?' said the girl with blue hair.

'This is wrong,' muttered Lori. 'This keeps on getting wronger and wronger. Jake?' she called to him from some twenty yards away. 'Jake, it's us. Lori and Bex.'

And at last he paused. Dark eyes regarded the girls coolly. 'What are you doing here? You shouldn't be here.'

'Nice,' grunted Bex. 'What happened to that legendary Midwestern hospitality?'

'You don't belong here,' Jake said by way of answer.

'Jake, we want to ask you some questions.' Lori ventured closer. So he recognised them at least. 'About when we were at Deveraux together.' Briefly she'd wondered about impersonation, physical reconstruction, but the black-haired boy before her now was Jake Daly all right. A holograph couldn't have produced a more faithful likeness.

'School's out,' said Jake. 'For ever.'

'We'll try not to keep you that long,' Bex assured him. 'But we were trying to remember, the college had a nickname, didn't it? We all used it, didn't we? Lo and I were racking our brains trying to think what it was, but we just couldn't. Thought you might remember it, Jake. Can you help us?'

Looked like not. Jake's features remained totally impassive, gave nothing away. 'You shouldn't be here. You know you shouldn't.'

'Do we? Why not? Who *says* not, Jake? Who?' For the first time he seemed confused. Lori went for it. 'We know about the mind-wiping.'

And the pickaxe nearly took her head off. 'Lo!' she heard Bex crying as she recoiled with injury-saving swiftness. She'd hoped to provoke a reaction, but not necessarily a homicidal one. Her ex-boyfriend swung the makeshift weapon again. Lori ducked below its hissing sweep. They'd argued at the end, yes, but she hadn't felt they'd parted on terms *this* bad.

Conclusion: contrary to appearances, this wasn't Jake.

'It's okay, Lo. I've got him!' Bex's wristband flashed in the false sun. The sleepshot shell drilled into the murderous Jake's back. It didn't even slow him down.

Conclusion: 'Blasted animates are everywhere!' complained Bex.

So Lori knew what she was up against, and it *was* a what, not a who. If she'd been wearing them, the gloves could have come off. Evading the latest stroke of the pickaxe, Lori reached for her mission belt instead, located what she needed without removing her eyes from her attacker for a second. Spy High agents in the field who couldn't multitask usually ended up immortalised in the Hall of Heroes. Lori had no intention of joining them.

The real Jake needed her.

The false Jake, however, was quickly outstaying his welcome. The pickaxe scythed downwards, keen to cut her in two. Lori sidestepped deftly, the deactivator in her hand. She jabbed out, slapped the small, spherical metal device against the animate's chest. It clung there like a limpet. Instantly, limbs froze and motion ceased. With a sound that might have been the electronic equivalent of a groan, the animate crashed to the ground.

Lori raised her eyebrows to her partner. 'Come back, Static Mode. All is forgiven.'

Bex knelt by the fallen assailant. 'Guess its command circuits couldn't cope with us turning up out of the blue and asking leading questions like that so it reverted to its basic self-preservation program.' She turned the body over and tapped it on the forehead. 'We're on to something, Lo. No way was Jake mind-wiped. If he had been, this would have been him, not an animate.'

'Obviously,' Lori said tetchily, scanning the empty fields. 'If he was ever here at all, he's not here now. So where is he, Bex? Where's Jake?'

THREE

From *The Secret Agent's Guide to the World*
by E.J. Grant
Appendix Two: Issues in Law Enforcement
(a) Incarceration

As the early decades of the twenty-first century passed, two trends of thinking regarding the treatment of antisocial elements developed, on the surface at least mutually irreconcilable. The execution of criminals had been banned worldwide as early as 2015, while what many saw as its legitimate replacement, the practice of carrying out brain implantations on deviant individuals to control their behaviour, was increasingly falling into disrepute with certain influential opinion-forming sections of the community as an affront to the subject's right to 'free thought'. Even if those free thoughts led to mass murder and terrorist atrocities, presumably. At the same time, however, fear of crime soared across the western world. Millions of people felt themselves to be under siege by those who held life and law in contempt, and they wanted something done. They demanded more visible security on their streets, more arrests, longer sentences. In the end, of course, the authorities had little choice but to respond, fearing that the voters might use their free thought to remove them from power come election time.

Inevitably, the prison population escalated. Massively. And without the twin tools of execution or radical surgery to keep its numbers under control, the system soon found that it could not cope. The construction of more prisons became a priority. But where to build them? The general public wanted criminals locked up, but they did not want to be living anywhere near those institutions where they *were* locked up.

The authorities searched both high and low for a solution, and found it in both directions. Penal satellites, orbiting the earth far beyond the sight of the taxpayers who had provided them. And the Deepwater Penitentiaries, the Aquatraz Agenda as it was dubbed by protesters, detainment facilities rooted to the bottom of the sea in America's offshore waters and accessed only by submarine.

At the time of writing, both building programmes seem to have retained the confidence and approval of the public. It appears that the

satellites and the Deepwaters will remain a
prominent feature of law enforcement policy for
a very long time to come.

The prisoners, like the animals, went in two by two, but
that was probably the only valid comparison between the
Deepwater One transfer submarine and Noah's Ark.

Certainly, the faces of the ranks of men and women in
drab grey uniforms were not indicative of gratitude for
being saved from a great calamity. Rather, the fixed
expressions of horror or hatred or despair suggested that
disaster lay only ahead.

'Keep moving! Keep moving!' The constant
command, barked by the guards in no-chances-taken
body armour who accompanied the condemned on their
way. Bawled by their comrades keeping watch from
raised platforms all along the route, pulse rifles at the
ready and trigger-fingers itching. Boomed by the crack-
lingly metallic tannoy system, direct from the vocal
cords of the Controller of Deepwater Transfer
Operations, the voice of God Himself.

The prisoners were marched along steel corridors on
opposite sides of the circular docking pool. Above them,
twenty storeys of holding cells and administrative offices,
a more voluntary form of incarceration, each one
hooping the air more tightly than the last, like a series of
ever-contracting handcuffs, until at the top, at the roof, a
mocking disc of glasteel and the unobtainable sky above.

'Take a look, crims,' one of the guards advised help-
fully. 'Take a good long look. That's the last you'll see of
the wide blue yonder for a while.'

There were different reactions to this unpleasant intelligence. Some cursed. Some groaned. One bleak soul actually laughed.

And the convict next to the black-haired youth decided to plead his innocence.

'I shouldn't be here. I've done nothing. It wasn't me. It was *them*.' He was an unshaven, dishevelled, twitching sort of man whose eyes seemed somehow too large for his head. 'I'm telling you, I'm innocent. I didn't kill those people. It was *them*.'

'You want to be more specific?' The black-haired youth was probably breaking the rules conversing with his hapless companion, but what were they going to do? Send him to jail?

'The aliens!' declared Bug-Eyes. 'They did it. They controlled me. They've been talking to me for years. They *forced* me.'

'Yeah, well they're talking to me too and they're telling you to shut up.'

'No talking there!' snapped a guard.

And then there was a howl, the kind of noise an animal might make if it could look between the slats of a truck, read the word Abattoir on the adjacent building, and know what it meant. For a convict a few pairs to the black-haired youth's rear, the prospect of life beneath the ocean had become more than he could bear. He made a break for it.

'Down! Down! Down!' The column of crims obeyed, dropping to the floor. There was a deafening fusillade of pulse-rifle blasts.

The howler had barely been able to step out of line.

He'd recover in time to settle into his new accommodation.

'On your feet, convicts! Keep moving! Keep moving!'

The submarine awaited. The loading continued.

The black-haired youth didn't miss a thing. His dark eyes darted in every direction, absorbing, recording, remembering, as if he was an official observer rather than a convicted prisoner. When the transfer sub was full and when it sank beneath the surface, its magnetic core energised, its reluctant passengers hammered at the hull with shouts and yells and the occasional ironic cheer. The black-haired youth remained silent. Alongside him, Bug-Eyes was sobbing quietly to himself. The black-haired youth ignored him and focused on the view beyond the porthole instead, waited for Deepwater One to put in an appearance.

When it did, it was impressive.

The penitentiary towered from the sand and rock of the seabed like a titanic lighthouse fashioned from metal and glasteel, a lighthouse long ago deluged and submerged but loyal to its service even now. Deep, dark waters swirled around its many levels, but from its peak strong beams of yellow light still bored through the flood, flashed against the transfer sub. As the arriving inmates watched, giant doors opened in the side of the structure, close to its summit, to allow their transport entry to the innards of Deepwater One, to the docking bay, to the processing area, to the cells.

The submarine was swallowed. The black-haired youth thought of Jonah in the belly of the whale. He was not the only one now who was mute.

They surfaced, the sub having to rise vertically into its bay. The prisoners were ordered outside in brisk, harsh tones. More guards, body-armoured, weapons to hand. In some ways, they might never have left the transfer base. Instructions for them to line up and to stand to attention. Pep-talk time.

'My name is Connell.' A man in the uniform of a chief security officer but whose features beneath his helmet were as hostile and brutal as those of many of his charges swaggered before them. 'You'll have plenty of time to learn it. Most of you are going to be with us for a while. You may address me as Chief Officer Connell or you may address me as sir, but I'd rather you didn't talk to me at all, or to anyone else, for that matter. I'd rather you remained as silent as you are now. Because let me give you a little piece of advice, my men and I like quiet convicts. We like convicts who keep themselves to themselves, who keep their heads down, who do what's requested of them promptly and efficiently and without complaint. We like convicts who serve out their sentences in a civilised way and who don't cause trouble.' Connell strutted along the line of prisoners, glaring at each of them in turn; none could return his gaze for long, or dared to. 'And let me tell you, you'll *want* my men and me to like you. You'll want it because down here, at the bottom of the sea, my men and I are the only authority there is, and we have the power to make your already wretched lives tolerable here in Deepwater One, or we can make them hell. It's your choice.' Connell paused in front of Bug-Eyes. 'What about you, little man? What kind of convict are you going to be?'

'I shouldn't be here, Officer Connell,' wailed Bug-Eyes pathetically.

'*Chief* Officer Connell,' snapped the guard. 'Not a good start. And what about you? Yes, you, next in line.'

'What about me, Chief Officer Connell?' said the black-haired youth mildly.

'Are you going to be the kind of convict who makes *noise*?' Fixing him with a glare.

'Only if and when specifically instructed to do so by yourself or a member of your staff, Chief Officer Connell,' said the black-haired youth, returning the stare steadily, unflinchingly, unafraid.

'Hmm. You're young to be sentenced to a Deepwater, aren't you, boy? What was your crime?'

'I burned some books, Chief Officer Connell,' came the admission. 'A library full, actually. And it seems some people were still reading them.'

'Then they've sent you to the right place, haven't they?' Connell grinned. 'Not so easy starting fires surrounded by millions of gallons of water.'

'So I understand, Chief Officer Connell. Could I ask, though, do they sell matches in the prison shop?'

The Chief Officer's expression hardened. 'You're getting loud, boy. What's your name?'

'Denver, sir,' the black-haired youth said. 'Jake Denver.'

And none of his former Bond Team partners were there to contradict him.

'Are you done yet?' fretted Lori.

'Nearly,' promised Bex.

The blonde girl peered nervously towards the horizon. So far, so wheat. 'Only we don't want Beth turning up or Jake's parents or anyone, do we? Explaining that the boy they thought was their brother and/or son is in fact a robot doppelganger designed to deceive them, well, I've got a feeling they wouldn't take the news too well. And it'd be pretty hard for them not to notice just at the minute.'

The Jake animate was sitting upright with its legs out-stretched and its hands in its lap. They were holding the top of its own head. Bex, meanwhile, was busy inside the rest of it. Sparks flared from within the skull as she worked.

'Nearly,' she repeated. 'As in almost, virtually, just about, not too long to go now. I'm not just swapping over a few plugs here, Lo. I'm deleting the last hour from this thing's memory circuits so when we put him on time-delayed reactivation mode, he'll have no recollection we were ever here.'

'Animate mind-wiping,' observed Lori wryly. 'Must run in the family.'

'Thanks for that,' said Bex. 'Not.'

'Sorry.' Lori came over and knelt by her friend. 'I'm just worried about Jake.'

'I know. We'll deal with it.' Bex squinted, applied the hand-held recalibrator to another of the animate's memory circuits. 'But first we have to get Jake II here functioning normally again.' She frowned fleetingly. 'It's not only the Dalys we have to keep in the dark about our little discovery.' More sparks. The whirr of reactivating machinery. 'There. That should do it. And the final touch . . .' She reached around the body, grabbed a thick shock of very human hair. 'Jake was never the type to lose his head.'

'That's the one good thing so far,' said Lori.

'What is?'

'We know Jake didn't lose control after all. It was an act. We know he didn't let anybody simply die.' Lori's relief curdled into self-reproach. 'I should have guessed this was some kind of deception from the moment we viewed that film.'

'How do you figure that?' said Bex. 'You weren't the only one fooled.'

'I was the only one who'd been as close to Jake as, well, as girlfriends get,' said Lori, a little self-consciously in Bex's presence. 'And he could have his black moods, sure. Sometimes there was a bitterness and a fury in him that threatened almost to take him over. When he saw the way killers and criminals worked the system, it maddened him. He could be difficult company then. But there were other times, truer, calmer times, times when Jake was warm and loving and giving. He could do more with his hands than form fists.'

'Oh, please, Lo,' cautioned Bex. 'Too much information.'

'Bex, what I'm trying to say is what I've always known and I should have let it guide me sooner. Jake could never kill anyone in cold blood.' Lori shook her head for emphasis. Her blonde hair was like gold. 'Only sometimes he needed someone to remind him that there's light in the world as well as dark.'

'Sounds like you're ready to reapply for the job, Lo,' remarked Bex.

'No.' A rueful smile. 'Too much water under the bridge. You can't go back. I'm with somebody else now, the guy I told you about. But what Jake and I had *was* special. *He's* special. And I've got a feeling he needs my help now more than ever.'

'Ditto that,' agreed Bex.

Lori gazed into the animate's unblinking eyes and sighed. 'Jake, what have you got yourself into?'

Of course, she might have had more of an idea had she been privy to the closing stages of Jake's interview with Jonathan Deveraux a few weeks earlier.

'They *want* to die. How can you fight that?' the teenager was protesting. 'How can you persuade a suicide bomber that he shouldn't detonate his bomb? *Unless* you're prepared to use whatever force is necessary to stop him.'

'Even *killing* force, Agent Daly?' Jake found he couldn't meet any of the founder's twenty-four eyes. 'But Deveraux agents do not kill.'

'No, sir.' But he didn't sound convinced.

'However,' said Jonathan Deveraux, 'secret agents who are not bound by the Deveraux organisation's rules need labour under no such limitation.'

'Sir?' What was Deveraux talking about?

'Do you remember this, Agent Daly?'

Other voices filled the room, recorded voices. Two of them, raised in heated argument. Familiar voices.

'No, Jake, that's not fair on either of us. We did the right thing. Sparing Lorenzo was the right thing.' Lori, pained and defensive.

'Oh, great. Cool. The *right thing*.' And himself, venomously sarcastic. 'If what we did was right, Lori, I'd hate to have a *wrong* thing on my conscience.'

He remembered. This exchange had taken place months ago. He and Lori, while they'd still been an item, had cornered a notorious drug baron, Miguel 'Mickey' Lorenzo, on his Bolivian estate. Lorenzo had been pushing a drug called rush. They learned he'd even got his own daughter addicted. Jake had held a shock blaster to the scumbag's head and had wanted to squeeze that trigger so *badly*. Thinking of scarred arms and scarred lives, so *badly*.

'Sir, how did you . . .?' Jake fumbled. 'Did you *tape* this or something?'

Lori had dissuaded him. Lori had used the old 'if we kill them we're the same as them' line, 'and we have to be better'. Because she was Lori and because he trusted her, Jake had conceded. Reluctantly, he'd let Lorenzo live.

'There is a saying in common parlance, is there not, Agent Daly?' said Deveraux. 'Walls have ears? Nothing that occurs within the walls of the college escapes my attention.'

And then Lorenzo had escaped from custody. Jake had given the due course of law the chance to prove itself, and it had let him down. Lorenzo would go on manufacturing and selling poison. Innocent kids would go on suffering. The due course of law was worthless. There had to be another way.

As Jake listened to the ghost voices of himself and Lori, the emotions of the original scene, played out a dozen floors below him now, returned. Maybe they'd never truly gone away. The anger. The frustration. The darkness descending.

'You *taped* us,' Jake said resentfully. 'A private conversation.'

'There is a greater good than the right to privacy, Agent Daly,' said Jonathan Deveraux. 'My actions serve it. So, I hope, will yours. Attend again to your own words.'

'You're happy with the way things are' – contemptuous of Lori in the past, while in the present wincing at how little she'd deserved it – 'playing chase with killers and madmen like the whole thing's a game, playing by the rules when the rules are stacked in the Bad Guy's favour. You're content with that. I'm not. I want new rules.' He remembered the final shake of his head, a gesture spitefully intended to hurt her. 'We're done.'

Fortunately, so was the recording. And Deveraux had *taped* them. That was bad. And he'd stored the moment like a much-loved CD. That was bad. And he'd chosen to play it to Jake alone now, today. Why?

'Do you still feel the same way, Agent Daly?' probed Deveraux. 'Are you still dissatisfied with our rules and with the justice system?'

'After sharing the skull of the subway bomber,' Jake snarled, 'in *spades*.'

'That is good,' said Jonathan Deveraux approvingly. 'My monitoring of your attitude and performance over the past two years predicted such a response. I have a proposition to put to you, Agent Daly.'

Jake felt his heart thudding. Change was coming. He felt it physically.

'The rise of the so-called apocalyptic terrorist has led me to conclusions similar to your own,' the founder explained. 'Those threats to world stability and order for whom the sanctions of the law contain no deterrent value whatsoever. To contain such threats, to eliminate them, Agent Daly, the old rules might need to be ignored. As you yourself said, we must fight by new rules, and I have concluded that the new rules are *no* rules. For the greater good, this must be so.'

'No rules.' Jake was beginning to feel he could maybe forgive Deveraux for eavesdropping on him and Lori before. It had been for the greater good, after all. And they had been speaking very loudly.

'I am authorising the deployment of a new breed of operative, Agent Daly, one that will still be able to utilise Deveraux's considerable resources, but one that at the same time will conduct covert counterterrorist missions outside the organisation's established parameters of engagement.'

'Black Ops,' breathed Jake, 'and licensed to kill.'

'Licensed to do whatever is necessary to combat the scourge of terrorism, Agent Daly, anything and everything.'

'And you want me to be one of these operatives, sir?' Just to clarify matters.

'You would be the first, Agent Daly. You would lead the way. But it must be your choice, because choices have consequences, and no agent undertaking missions of this nature can possibly remain officially associated with the Deveraux organisation. Our continued good relations with certain governments and other international bodies would be jeopardised, and that cannot be allowed to happen.'

'So what would I have to do? Resign?' Jake conjectured. 'I mean, if I *did* want in on the Black Ops deal, what would it mean for me first?'

'It would mean turning your back on the life you have known since you entered the Deveraux College at the age of fourteen,' admitted Jonathan Deveraux. 'It would mean leaving behind you your friends and partners, deceiving them, too. None could know about your new role.'

Jake frowned. 'How would that be possible?'

'There are ways.' Deveraux seemed unworried. 'But first, you must decide. Will you be a part of this new initiative? Will you match your words with actions?'

Sounded like a challenge to Jake. Would he rise to it? *Should* he? He thought of the nameless subway terrorist. He thought of Mickey Lorenzo. He thought of Tepesch and Talon and Frankenstein and all the other major scumbags Bond Team had faced and fought over the years. And he thought of their victims, all the lives they hadn't been able to save, all the screams they hadn't been able to still. The thing about Bad Guys, the Moriarty Syndrome, their teachers called it, was they always came back. Unless you blew the top of Moriarty's head off. That would stop him in his tracks. That would save lives. And that was what Jake was in this business for, wasn't it? Not the glory, like maybe Ben. Not the belonging, like Cally. Not to prove himself, like Lori or Bex.

Not because nowhere else would have him, like Eddie. To save lives. And if he could do so by slightly redirecting his own life, wouldn't that be worth it? Wouldn't that be good?

'What is your decision, Agent Daly?' prompted Jonathan Deveraux.

He'd miss the others, but if they knew what he was doing and why, he hoped they'd understand.

'I'm in, sir,' he said.

'Good,' acknowledged Deveraux. 'Then we can begin. And we will do so by assigning you a code-name in keeping with your new status. You are Agent Daly no more. Now you are Jake Black.'

The cells at Deepwater One were pretty much the same as cells elsewhere, except for the bars on the windows. There weren't any. Jake supposed there didn't need to be. The reinforced glasteel squares offered vistas of murky depths and crushing pressures only. Unless a convict possessed gills instead of lungs, there was no escape for him in that direction.

They were two-man cells (or two-woman: sexual equality had even found its way into the penal system). At first Jake was grateful he wasn't having to share his accommodation with Bug-Eyes ('I must have the top bunk. The aliens are *commanding* me to take the top bunk'). At *first*.

'Who are you?' demanded the weasely man with the narrow, suspicious face.

'I guess I'm your new cellmate,' Jake said. 'Jake Denver.'

He put out his hand, which the weaselly man inspected as if it was something dead and crawling with maggots.

'You think you're better than me?'

Jake was taken aback. 'Sorry?'

'Do you think you're better than me?' The man thrust his weaselly head closer to Jake. It reached his chin. ' 'Cause you're younger and taller and stronger. Do you think that makes you better than me?'

'Ah, well actually I haven't given it any thought at the moment.' Come back, Bug-Eyes, Jake begged, all is forgiven.

'Only my classmates, they all thought they were better than me. Better-looking. Better prospects. Better lives. They thought they were so clever. They laughed at me at high school.'

'Yeah, well, kids can be cruel like that.' Jake hoped he at least *sounded* sympathetic.

'They're not laughing now, though.'

'Are they not?'

The weaselly man exposed teeth like broken fencing. 'At their tenth-anniversary reunion, I made it go with a *bang*.' Considerately adding a sound effect. 'You think you're better than me?'

'Absolutely not.' Best not to antagonise the little lunatic, not while there was a mission to complete. 'As far as I'm concerned, this is your cell. You're the man. I'm just like a junior partner, okay?'

The weaselly man seemed to think it okay. 'Bugby,' he said.

'You've lost me.'

'Soren Bugby.' Eyes narrowing. 'You think your name's—'

'It's a really great name. Really. I wish I had one just like it.'

The weaselly man was placated. 'Let me introduce you to Aquatraz,' he said.

The Grand Tour wasn't exactly necessary. Jake had already been thoroughly briefed on the geography and operational practices of Deepwater One, but he deemed it advisable to humour Soren Bugby, at least for the time being.

The penitentiary was actually quite easy to negotiate. Circular floors, following the lighthouse model, wider at the base then narrowing. Twenty-five of them. Organised in a rigid hierarchy. At the bottom, the prisoners' quarters. The lowest level of all, scraping the seabed itself, contained the punishment cells. Moving up, the solitaries and then the regular lockups, those for females arcing around one half of Deepwater's circumference, those for males around the other. At the centre of the prisoner accommodation levels, a huge hollow shaft, bisected by twin glasteel elevators. These were for the use of prison security officers only and dropped from the heights of the building to its depths, connected by bridges to each landing. The inmates themselves also used elevators to transfer from one floor to another, but these were shackled to the walls and constantly monitored from the prison control centre: they were fitted with a number of sanction devices to discourage bad behaviour on the part of their occupants, for example electroshock floors and walls and gas-jets that could render even the most recalcitrant of cons unconscious inside three seconds.

But continuing up through the body of Deepwater One. Above the cells, the recreational levels, the exercise level, the mess hall, the infirmary, a sense of ascension to a better place. Then the prison's administrative levels, the floors where the guards had their rooms and entertainment facilities – it was rumoured a bar. Finally, like a mountain peak, like the summit of aspiration, like the promise of Heaven, the control centre, the seat of power in Deepwater One. Everything was operated from the control centre, including the penitentiary's emergency evacuation subs and that holy of holies, the only possible way out of Aquatraz, the docking bay.

Needless to say, of course, Soren Bugby could not show his cellmate these latter levels personally. They got as far as the mess hall.

'Where we eat,' Jake was informed.

'Yeah?' He nodded with a degree of enthusiasm normally reserved for great revelations. The sight of prisoners hunched over long tables and gobbling greedily from steel trays had, however, already kind of given the secret of the room away.

'Most of us,' said Soren Bugby resentfully. 'You may not be aware of it, Denver, but we have a celebrity in our midst.'

'Yeah?' Innocent interest.

'Null. He's one of these terrorists, one of these Bringers of the Night.'

'I think I've heard of him,' said Jake. *Why I'm here, you sick runt.*

'Bringer of airs and graces more like,' Bugby seethed. 'Thinks he's better than the rest of us. Too good to eat in the mess hall. Has his meals in his cell. He's a solitary, special case, gets his own cell, doesn't have to share, too good to share, and I hear he gets his own way in other things too.'

'Yeah?'

'Visitors. Special privileges. Because he claims he's a political prisoner.' Bugby spat. 'He's a killer like the rest of us. He's no better.'

'I bet he's not even as good,' encouraged Jake. For the first time, it seemed Bugby might have information he could use. 'So does Null never come out of his cell?'

'For exercise period,' Bugby said. 'Joins us then. Thinks he's better than us, though. Looks down his nose. I'd like to show him. People who think they're better than me, I hate 'em . . .'

Jake had kind of gathered that. 'So why haven't you?'

Bugby's eyes flitted from side to side like flies looking for somewhere to settle. 'He's got friends. He's got influence.'

'With the guards?'

'With the guards. With the cons. He talks. About darkness. About night. He talks like he knows more than us, like he's cleverer. He talks like he's got answers, like what he says means something. *I* know it's all just words but some of the cons listen, some of them *follow*.'

'What do you mean?' Jake frowned.

'They look up to him. They join him. They say they believe in the Bringers of the Night. They believe in this Sicarius Null says he serves and they believe in *him*.' Bugby clenched his fists. 'I'd show them. I'd prove Null's nothing, but there's always his followers around him. You can't get to him unless you get through *them*.'

'Is that right?' pondered Jake.

'She's one of them there.' The weaselly man stabbed a finger towards a table as viciously as if it had been a dagger. 'Her. She's one of them. *Dark*.'

'What?' Jake examined the target of Bugby's attention. A girl, yes, his own age or maybe a little older. ('Young to be sentenced to a Deepwater.' He remembered Connell's words to him. 'What was your crime?')

'Dark. It's what she calls herself. Not exactly a looker, is she?' Almost gleefully.

And almost accurately. The girl maybe wouldn't be challenging Lori for Cheerleader of the Year, not with her hair such an uncertain brown as that and kind of clumped on her head as it was, and maybe not with her teeth quite as prominent or her freckles quite so many. And yet, Jake thought, in her *eyes*. The windows of the soul, he'd always been told. There was potential in the green of Dark's eyes.

If only to further his mission.

And she might never be a pin-up person, but that didn't seem to be putting off a pair of possible suitors. A man with a head like a potato with the eyes intact. Another whose skin seemed to be sagging from his face like old sacking. They'd taken advantage of empty seats on either side of her. Now they appeared to be keen to take advantage of Dark herself.

Jake couldn't have planned a better opening if he'd tried. 'Excuse me for a moment, will you, Soren?'

'Where you goin'?'

'It's time for my exercise period.'

The two crims were pressing themselves against her. In language as salty as the sea outside, Dark was raising issues of personal space with them. Feisty. Jake liked that. But the crims weren't listening. Potato-Head's fingers had gone walkabout on Dark's arm. Her teeth clenched in revulsion.

Seconds out, Jake thought.

'I think the hands'd be better occupied with the cutlery, don't you?'

Potato-Head looked up at Jake standing on the other side of the table. A stupid malice creased his features. 'Who the hell are you?'

'I'm the guy who's asking you and your unfortunate friend to leave the lady alone and go sit somewhere else.'

'New boy,' guessed Potato-Head. 'New boy, you're messing with the wrong man.'

'This is the mess hall, isn't it?' Jake was grinning. Then he wasn't. 'Hands. Off. Now.'

'Or what?' sneered Potato-Head.

'Or somebody else is going to have to feed you.'

Nudges at either end of the table. Whispers. Glances. Spreading through the mess hall like germs. The residents of Deepwater One knew fighting talk when they heard it. It was about the only genuine source of entertainment they had.

Potato-Head's lips parted as if somebody had taken his resemblance to the tuber literally and was beginning to peel him. 'Okay, okay,' he conceded. 'Have it your own way.' Fingers on fork. *'Punk!'*

Jake was ready. Even as Potato-Head thrust to his feet and stabbed with the fork he was in position. Swaying aside, he seized the man's arm and pulled. The table between them helped. It was fixed to the floor in order to prevent its use as a weapon on occasions such as this. It jabbed into Potato-Head's gut and winded him. His food-piled tray skittered forward. Jake flattened its owner's face into it. 'Eat up. Make you a nice strong boy.'

Cheers and roars of approval from the cons. Fists thumping on tabletops The guards stationed around the perimeter of the mess hall stirred.

Sagging-Skin was on the table. 'You little . . .' Leaping at Jake.

The attack was telegraphed so early the teenager could have seen it coming the day before. Why get involved when you could sidestep trouble just as easily? Sagging-Skin crashed into the diners on the next table. They weren't happy. They were distinctly unhappy. They swung punches at Sagging-Skin and they connected. But not necessarily with the original culprit. A more general fight broke out. Someone somewhere smacked a tray over his neighbour's head. The gesture was reciprocated. It caught on.

The guards found themselves wading into a full-scale brawl.

Only Dark did not participate. Which at least meant it

would be easier for Jake to talk to her. 'Hi,' he said, sitting opposite. 'Jake Denver.'

'Where?'

'No, that's me. Here. I'm Jake Denver. Hi.'

'I wish I was.'

Kind of easier to talk to her. 'I think the custom is, I tell you my name, you tell me yours.' He tapped his chest. 'Jake Denver.' Thought tapping hers might be a little presumptuous. 'It's Dark, isn't it? My cellmate told me. Actually, he's not really my mate but you know what I mean.' He was looking her in the eye but getting nowhere. The windows to Dark's soul were shuttered up and boarded over. 'You don't have to speak if you don't want to. You know, just blink. Once for yes, twice for no. Is your name Dark?'

'What do you want?' the girl glowered.

'A word of thanks, maybe. It could only be one syllable. You know, for saving you from the dribbling attentions of the Missing Link twins back there.'

'So you could move in yourself?' With supreme contempt. Jake flinched involuntarily. 'I don't think so. In fact, I'll tell you what I was about to tell them before I was so gallantly interrupted.' She plucked up her knife and flourished it above her shoulder as if she was auditioning for a slasher movie, and not as the victim. Her loose grey sleeve slid to her elbow. Jake saw the scars seaming her arm like woodcuts. 'Any man comes near me – or *boy* – I'll make him wish he'd never been born.'

A battered convict slammed face down on the table between them. Someone seemed to have turned the volume up on the cacophonous chaos of riot. Yells and howls and a screeching laughter, maybe from Bugby. A madhouse. The whole place was a madhouse.

For maybe the first time, Jake wondered what he'd got himself into.

FOUR

'**B**ugby claims the incident was sparked off by Michaels and Eleziak,' Chief Officer Connell told him. 'So does Dark. Therefore, Denver, I have decided to give you the benefit of the doubt. No further disciplinary action will be taken. But I warn you, you would be wise to be quieter in future. You've scarcely arrived in Deepwater and already you're starting to make yourself heard.'

'Yes, Chief Officer Connell, sir,' Jake said, demonstrating the expected gratitude impeccably. 'Thank you, sir.' And Dark had spoken up for him, had she? Maybe he'd made more of an impression on her than the girl had liked to admit.

On the other hand, 'I'd keep well away from her, Denver,' advised Soren Bugby in their cell. 'All of them Bringers of the Night types. They think they're better than us. She was never a normal girl anyway, that Dark. Not 'cording to what I've heard.'

'What have you heard, Soren?'

'The Beauty Salon Burner, that was one name they called her. The Cosmetics Killer was another. Torched a trail of beauty parlours and physical reconstruction clinics halfway across the country. Guess the poor folks caught in them at the time called her something else, don't you? Give the likes of her the tongue, boy, she'll bite it off.'

But Jake reckoned Bugby was exaggerating. He had seen the scars on Dark's pale skin and knew what they signified. The Beauty Salon Burner was likely to be of greater danger to herself than to others. It was elementary psychology, a first-term job at Spy High along with weapons maintenance, basic kung fu, and hacking into the Pentagon's computer system: those who harmed themselves hated themselves. Dark's problems, Jake estimated, were almost certainly rooted in a lack of self-esteem. Also made her easy prey, a perfect recruit for cultish groups like the Bringers of the Night, groups that purported to offer the lost, lonely individual refuge and relief in an entity and a cause larger than him- or herself.

He was beginning to feel a certain sympathy for Dark until he remembered the subway bomber: maybe that murdering piece of filth would have offloaded the responsibility for his atrocities on to an unhappy childhood too, a mother who didn't love him, a father who wasn't there. Excuses. These days crims always had excuses. Jake felt his hands forming fists. In the end, you were responsible for your own actions, your own life choices. You and no one else. Whatever they were.

And if you chose to be a terrorist, then Jake Black was coming for you.

The next day he saw Null in the flesh for the first time.

Exercise periods in Deepwater One were, as might be imagined, somewhat different from other prisons. There was no yard, no access to open air, no tantalising glimpse of freedom beyond the wall. Instead, the techs who'd designed Aquatraz had equipped its vast exercise chamber, occupying an entire level, with hologram capability. So twice a day it appeared to the wretched inmates that they'd miraculously returned to the surface. It seemed that they were strolling on grass, and that clouds were scudding across the sky above them, and that a light breeze was stroking the leaves of the distant trees like a hand on a lover's hair. All false, obviously, all an illusion, and Jake wasn't sure whether to remind the condemned of what they were missing so vividly indicated compassion or cruelty.

He didn't have a great deal of time to consider the matter. Bugby had been right concerning Null's participation in exercise periods. He'd also been right about how the Bringer never walked alone.

Null first. A man of about forty, a similar age to his leader, Sicarius. In every other respect, however, the two terrorists seemed to have little in common. Jake had viewed all the archive material available, and where Sicarius was tall and imposing, Null was of average height if not a little stooped. Where Sicarius' hair was blind man's black, Null's was an undistinguished brown. And where the leader's bone structure was perfect for sculpture, the lieutenant's was unlikely to attract the attention of artists. Physically, Null would never stand out in a crowd; he could be anyone. Yet there was one quality that he and Sicarius did appear to share, and it was sufficient for Jake to file his fellow prisoner under Extremely Dangerous. It was the malevolence, the loathing for life, the contempt for the surrounding world that radiated from him like a conquering force, a total absence of pity or humanity, announcing that here was a man who would kill without question, kill without mercy, kill without stopping.

Jake detected the same callousness in his followers, too, the several-strong entourage of men – and one girl – who clustered around him, protecting him. A black guy with a shaven head seemed to be prominent, but it was Dark who intrigued him most.

What was she doing with scum like that? She didn't belong with Null. Impossible. She wasn't a Bringer of the Night. Jake assured himself he wasn't allowing sentimentality to cloud his judgement because of her sex. Female fingers could pull a trigger or press a detonator just as easily as male. No, it wasn't that. It was the kind of sad way she seemed to be hovering on the margins of the group, like someone who was tolerated but not really liked. For some reason Jake was pleased. And the ruthless, brutal aura that emanated from the others, he did not sense it in her. She was *with* them, but not one *of* them.

Jake began to feel sympathy again. To a point. It wouldn't stop him using her. It couldn't. Because watching how his acolytes kept the other cons at a respectful –

and harmless – distance from the Bringer as he practically processed through the exercise chamber, Jake realised something else. Bugby's assessment of the difficulties of getting close to Null was on the button as well. Dark was his only option.

It was lucky that even in the penal system, meals came three times a day.

'You don't give up, do you?' the girl said as Jake placed his tray opposite hers and sat down.

'You haven't threatened to run me through with your dinner knife yet so I must be getting somewhere,' Jake replied.

Dark scoffed. 'You're not worth a week in the punishment cells, that's all.'

'Anyway, I wanted to thank you. For speaking up for me to Connell. Telling him it wasn't me who started that ruck the other day.'

Dark shrugged. 'If that's it you can move along, Jake Denver. That fancy-a-dance grin you seem to be afflicted with is making me nauseous, and it's hard enough keeping this slop down at the best of times. Go on, get lost. I've got nothing you want.'

'Actually, you have.' Jake leaned forward conspiratorially. 'I want to join the Bringers of the Night.'

Dark seemed to lose what little appetite she had, pushed her tray to one side. 'Is that right?'

'I know you're one of them. I've seen you with Null during exercise period. I thought maybe you could introduce me. I've got talents. I can follow orders. I can contribute.'

' 'Fraid it doesn't work like that,' Dark said. 'Even if I

wanted to help you out, which I don't, you don't just *choose* to join the Bringers. They choose *you*. Why don't you join the prison's poetry appreciation group instead? I'm betting that's more your style.'

She looked like she was about to stand and leave. Jake couldn't allow that.

'So let's just talk about you instead,' he tried.

'I don't think so.' Still getting to her feet.

'Why? Don't you think you're worth talking about?'

He'd struck a nerve. Dark was glaring at him, but she was pausing. Then she was resuming her seat like a sullen student called back by a teacher. 'What do you think you know about me?'

'I don't know anything,' Jake said, 'but I want to. I think you're interesting.'

Dark laughed bitterly. 'You think I'm easy. You think I'd be grateful. Ugly girls have got to be grateful when boys come calling.'

'Who says you're' – Jake baulked at repeating it precisely – 'not good-looking?'

Dark's teeth protruded even further. 'The world. But okay, let's assume I'm deluded temporarily by your sunshine smile and cut-price flattery. Genie out of the bottle kind of thing. You get three questions.'

'What's your real name?' said Jake.

'Dark *is* my real name.'

'Did you really torch those salons? I heard—'

'You heard right. Up in smoke they went. Whoosh.' Dark's fingers made fire above the table.

'Why?'

And she winked. 'Because it was worth it.'

'But what about the people inside? Didn't you care about them?'

'That's questions four and five,' Dark seized on Jake's presumption, 'so they're coming straight back at you. What *about* the people inside? Did *they* care about *me*?' She rose. 'Food's getting cold, Jake. That gravy's gonna congeal if you're not careful. See ya.'

This time he let her go without protest. She'd given him enough to think about for one mealtime. Because he'd been wondering incredulously as she spoke how someone as young as Dark could be so heartless, so cold-blooded about the taking of human life. Until it occurred to him.

Wasn't Jake Black now expected to be the same?

His final briefing had taken place after the charade of his mind-wipe. Agent Daly was dead, he thought. Long live Jake Black. But he was glad that he hadn't been forced to see his partners' faces as he'd been cuffed into the chair and the memory adjustment helmet lowered, the one that didn't actually do anything but buzz a bit and look impressively technological. It would have been nearly impossible not to give the game away even at that late stage if he'd been subject to the hurt and bewilderment in Lori's blue eyes. He'd almost betrayed himself back on the rooftop, just before she'd shot him. Deceiving the Bad Guys, Jake could handle that. He relished it. They *deserved* to be duped. But making fools of his friends, well, he wasn't proud of himself over *that* aspect of what he was doing.

Just as well the Greater Good outweighed everything.

The briefing was held not, for obvious reasons, at Spy High, but at one of the Deveraux safe-houses that lay hidden behind the façades of otherwise ordinary houses in otherwise ordinary streets in every major country of the world. There was Jake. There was Jonathan Deveraux, his holographic head, at least. There was a tech reassigned to the Black Ops division.

And there was Sicarius, rising from the holo-scape like civilisation's bogeyman. His piercing eyes, his malignant sneer, every aspect of his appearance designed for dread.

'Sicarius claims that the Bringers of the Night are a religious group,' Jonathan Deveraux said, 'but it seems they take a novel interpretation of the Creation story. How is your knowledge of Genesis, Agent Black?'

'Weren't they a twentieth-century prog rock band, sir? Peter Gabriel, Phil . . .' Jonathan Deveraux was not renowned for his sense of humour. 'Sorry, sir. I guess you mean the Book of Genesis, the first book of the Christian Bible. God creating the world in six days and resting on the seventh. He wouldn't get away with that with Sunday trading laws nowadays, would He? Adam and Eve. Cain and Abel. Noah.'

'Too far, Agent Black,' said Deveraux. 'Only the opening verses are relevant.' And the disembodied head recited them: 'In the beginning, when God created the Universe, the Earth was formless and desolate. The raging ocean that covered everything was engulfed in total darkness, and the power of God was moving over the water. Then God commanded, "Let there be light." And there was light. And God saw that it was good.'

Jake remembered the ancient words from childhood

Sunday school, though more often than not he'd been gazing out of the window wondering exactly when God had found time to create the Dome and, more saliently, why he'd bothered.

'Let there be light, Agent Black,' said Jonathan Deveraux. 'The original command. The commencement of all things. And since the beginning our culture has celebrated light, sought its brilliance, savoured it, cherished it. The light of understanding, of learning, of knowledge. The light of beauty, the radiance of purity and truth. The light of life itself. In our history, in our art, in the souls of men, light has always been worthy of attainment in all its forms.

'The Bringers of the Night, however, see things differently. For Sicarius and his acolytes, light is evil, an enemy to be despised. What has light done, they accuse, except to illuminate human flaws and sins and imperfections, to force exposure on what would be better kept secret and dark? Light blinds men to the truth, they say, the truth that only darkness is the path to peace. The Bringers believe in black, and the cause they embrace as holy is to bestow the blessing of eternal night, of unending, perfect oblivion, on everyone.'

'That's death, right, sir?' Jake frowned. 'Their twisted minds think they're doing people a favour by killing as many as possible, including themselves if that's what it takes.' He scowled at Sicarius. 'You're sick, man, you know that?'

'Your diagnosis may be psychologically accurate, Agent Black,' conceded Jonathan Deveraux. 'Nevertheless, this is the nature of our foe. For Sicarius and the Bringers of the Night, the coming of light marked the beginning of mankind's woes. If they could, they would return the world to the void before creation, when all was formless and desolate, and darkness held dominion.'

'Well,' Jake considered grimly, 'at least there's not much chance of that.'

'Your mission, Agent Black, is to ensure that Sicarius is rendered incapable of committing further outrages of any kind.'

'Sounds good to me, sir. It's just a shame he's not in the phone book.'

'You will be placed in the same prison as his lieutenant, Null,' Deveraux elaborated. 'You will earn the trust of this Null and profess a desire to join the Bringers of the Night. You will learn from him how to locate Sicarius and then you will do so.'

'Yes, sir.' Jake was liking this. Jake was up for it.

'Then, when you are standing by the terrorist's side,' Deveraux said without emotion, 'you will kill him.'

As soon as the Dome was out of sight behind them, Lori and Bex landed their SkyBikes by the side of the road.

'Okay,' reminded Bex. 'As planned. I'll use both channels of my bike's comlink to contact Cally and Ben. You try Eddie.'

'You say that like it's a short straw, Bex,' chided Lori. 'What's Eddie ever done to you?'

'Nothing,' said Bex. 'I wouldn't let him.'

'It'd be easier if we put in the calls from Spy High.'

'Easier for Dad to monitor them too,' Bex said grimly. 'No chances, Lo. The only people I trust right now are you and the others. Which is why we need them. Remember our Bond Team motto? All for one and one for all.'

'That wasn't us. That was the Three Musketeers.'

'You're so picky, Lori, did anyone ever tell you that?' She rapped the comlink on her bike. 'Hey, Benjamin White, Calista Green. Wakey wakey.'

'Heads up,' alerted Lori. 'Company.'

A Mark Four wheelless, red, shiny and new, drew up to a hover alongside the Deveraux agents. The Mark Fours were nicknamed Fourraris. They were very fast and very expensive. The male driver retracted the roof so the girls could get a better look at him. They saw mainly teeth, a different colour to the wheelless but just as shiny and probably just as new.

'Great,' grumbled Bex. 'Here we go again.' Mouthing the words mockingly: 'Hey, gorgeous, need any help?'

'Hey, beautiful,' the teeth gleamed at Lori, 'need any help?'

'Gorgeous. Beautiful. Whatever,' muttered Bex.

'No thanks.' Lori's teeth were equally white but a little more natural.

'Only I've got plenty of room inside if you need a ride.'

'Inside your *head*, sleazebag.' Under her breath.

'No, we're fine.' Lori was adamant. 'Thanks.'

'Say, haven't I seen you in one of those fashion magazines?' the teeth seemed to think. 'Sure I have. Aren't you a model?'

'Not so far,' said Lori.

'Well you ought to be. Listen, I know some people . . .'

'Hey, hey!' Bex had had enough. 'Am I invisible here or what?'

'If only,' said the teeth. 'Who are you, darling? The daughter of Dorothy and the Tin Man? Bet it's fun getting you through airport security.'

'Are those dentures of yours insured against damage caused in roadside accidents?' Bex said. ' 'Cause it's a policy you're gonna be needing like real soon.'

'Bex,' intervened Lori, 'don't let an idiot like this goad you.'

'Who is she, beautiful?' the teeth enquired. 'Some retard Domer cousin or something?'

'She's a friend,' said Lori. 'Unlike you. Now weren't you driving that way?'

The teeth glanced between the two girls, uttered a ribald laugh. 'If that's how you want it, beautiful. It's your loss.'

'I'll try to get over it,' Lori assured him. 'Remember to brush after every meal now, y'hear?'

The wheelless blurred red to the horizon like a smear of lipstick.

'If you find yourself wishing someone has a wheelless accident and smashes up their brand-new Fourrari, Lori,' Bex postulated, 'does that make you a bad person?'

Lori shook her head. 'Forget him.'

'How do you do it, though, Lo?'

'How do I do what?'

'Get guys falling at your feet like that. Wherever we go it happens.'

'Regular pedicures help,' Lori grinned, 'but get real, Bex, you're not telling me you'd be happier having sleazes like that coming on to you instead of me, are you?

Let me tell you, leers across the room are no substitute for a proper relationship.'

'As I get neither,' Bex confessed, 'can't really make a comparison.'

'What? Well whose fault is that? You have to look harder, Bex.'

'You mean like with optical implants?'

'I mean like with an open mind. There are guys out there for you.' Lori gave a general sweep with her arm that seemed to include half the country.

'Exactly!' Bex declared. 'They're out there and I'm here and . . .' The comlink on her bike was flashing for attention. 'Looks like the love-life discussion'll have to wait, Lo. We have . . .' She was going to say 'contact', but when she saw the nature of the signal that the comlink was in fact receiving, the word suddenly lost its appropriateness. 'Greensign,' she reported disappointedly. 'And whitesign. What about Eddie?'

'The same,' sighed Lori from her bike. 'Redsign only.'

'So. Scratch Plan A.' Bex slumped back in her saddle. The information on their comlinks told the girls only one thing. Calista Green, Benjamin White and Edward Red were all currently on active mission status. They could not be contacted until operations were completed, and there was no knowing when that would be. A Deveraux agent's code-sign was notoriously tight-lipped. In short, their former team-mates were out of the picture.

'I guess we move to Plan B then,' suggested Lori.

'Yep,' agreed Bex. 'Looks like finding Jake is down to us.'

❋

Another day, another exercise period. Null with Dark and the rest of his followers on one side of the chamber, casting disapproving glances at the holo-sun in the bright blue sky and doubtless wishing that night would fall – permanently. Jake and Bugby loitering on the other.

Jake too was wondering whether Plan A might not be defunct.

Dark was hiding behind so many barriers that if she was a miner trapped by a cave-in it would take the rescue party a week to break through to her, and by then of course she'd have suffocated. Jake was therefore torn. Either he had to work faster than that or abandon the girl to her fate. It was a matter of priorities: which was more important, Dark or the mission? Wasn't even a question.

But he'd give her one final chance. The Bringers must have noticed him and Bugby entering the chamber. He fixed his eyes on Dark. If he'd made any impact on her at all, if there was any possibility of her mentioning him to Null, the back that was presently turned to him like a closed door would relent. She'd turn round. She'd look for him, at him, like someone peeping through the curtains of a lonely house.

'Did you hear me, Denver?'

Now Bugby was one person he'd be happy to see the back of, in more ways than one. 'What was that, Soren?' *Come on, Dark. Do it. Look at me.*

'I said you're all right by me.'

She did it. She turned. Their eyes met. There was startlement in hers that his should be waiting for her, then something that might have been fear. Jake wasn't given long enough to judge. She was shunning him again. A glance of a second, and no second glance. It didn't matter. It was enough.

In mission terms, Plan A was still on track.

'What was that, Soren?' Jake felt suddenly bursting with good humour. 'You think I'm all right? That makes me feel kind of warm inside, you know?'

'Only when you first came' – this qualified as a deep emotional confession from Bugby – 'you looked a bit like you thought you were better than me . . .'

Dark had pushed past the black guy with the shaven head, had insinuated herself next to Null. She was talking to him. Jake hoped he was the subject.

'. . . and we wouldn't have got on then. Sooner or later, I'd have had to kill you . . .'

Distantly, scarcely registering Bugby's words: 'Is that right, Soren?' Because Jake was noticing others with an apparent interest in the Bringers of the Night.

'. . . But I was wrong. You don't think you're someone you're not, Denver . . .'

They'd been knotted together earlier. Now they'd broken up. Half a dozen of them. Hardened crims. Nothing-to-lose types. Born in a brawl. Not the kind ordinarily to work in a team, but they were united now. Slowly, subtly, they were surrounding Null's group. Insidiously, inexorably, they were closing in.

'. . . so I just wanted to say—'

Just as Jake's Deveraux-honed senses had singled the crims out for attention, so they now anticipated what was coming next. Inevitably.

'Not now, Soren. There's going to be trouble.'

Confirmed. Hands thrust into pockets. Eyes sparking like flints. The hint of a blade.

The guards chatting blandly at their posts.

Null's Bringer bodyguards, unaware of what was happening, of what was *going* to happen.

Null wouldn't be telling him where to find Sicarius with his throat cut.

It was a beautiful day in the exercise chamber of Deepwater One.

'Watch out!' Jake yelled.

Roars from the crims as they drew their knives.

A beautiful day. But it wouldn't last.

FIVE

Jake hammered into the first crim's back. It was solid, like timber. As the man pitched forward Jake used it as a vault, launched himself nearer to Null, to Dark.

It was pretty obvious to the entire exercise chamber what was going on now.

Null's followers were galvanised, encircled him quickly, prepared to defend him. Shaven-Head barking belated orders. The prison alarm jangled like a hysterical woman. The guards, to be fair, moved in to end the disturbance. Found they weren't allowed to. The inmates not immediately involved blocked their path. It had been a while since there'd been the prospect of violence as deadly as this outbreak promised. They didn't want to spoil it.

Chief Officer Connell wasn't going to be happy. Too much *noise*.

Cries. Shouts. Obscenities brandished like guns. The thud and thump and crack and crunch of fists and boots inflicted with savage intent on the bodies of others. The whistle of air cut open by crudely crafted blades, the slash and slice. The gasps and groans of pain.

Sounds that Jake had come to know well, as he knew too how to cope with them. Ignore them. They were background, they were inadvisable distraction. They were the muzak of mayhem. Focus on actions, not the sound they made, and the actions that would remove the threat of your opponent and keep you alive.

If the crim with the knife was thrusting high, drop low. If he'd got weight, and a lot of it, even if most of it was muscle, use it against him. If he was charging forward, even directly at you, help him on his way. If his legs were visible, sweep them with one of your own. But get out of the way before he fell.

The floor of the chamber seemed springy with grass, but it was concrete.

The prisoners were no match for Jake. The successful fighter was the clever fighter, and these jerks had more convictions than brain cells. Even in the midst of mêlée, he had time to look for Dark.

Who may not have been hungry before, but who seemed to be making up for it now. A pockmarked crim howled as the wild girl with the freckles gnawed on his forearm. His home-made dagger fell from his grip. He retaliated by yanking on Dark's hair with his other hand. She lost her grip in turn, was tugged back. A gap opened between them. Jake took advantage.

'Pulling a girl's hair. Didn't anyone ever tell you that's bad form?' His scissor kick sent spittle spraying from the crim's mouth. 'I'd see someone about that saliva problem too. When you wake up.'

'I don't need your help, Denver,' Dark was remarking acidly. 'I can handle myself.'

'*You?*' Jake retorted, he hoped with convincing scorn. 'I'm watching out for *Null.*'

Who throughout the battle had stood as calm and unflustered as if he wasn't its focus, as if it wasn't even happening. And maybe the worst was over. Security reinforcements were arriving, beating inmates aside, dragging them from the chamber and no doubt to their cells. Connell was ordering a lock-down. The prospective assassins were not going to reach Null now. Except . . .

One man had bided his time. An older man, a seasoned con, hair grey where it remained at all. He'd somehow managed to edge close to Null. With Shaven-Head occupied in pounding another attacker into pulp, he and Sicarius' lieutenant were almost face to face. The Bringer was smiling faintly. Even when from inside his regulation issue shirt the con produced a shock blaster. He hadn't knocked that up in the penitentiary's workshop, Jake realised. *Someone* wanted Null dead.

But the man himself didn't seem to mind. He was motionless still. He was studying the blaster with amused indifference. Perhaps he thought it time to embrace oblivion.

Maybe later. For the moment at least, Jake needed him alive.

He moved like lightning, struck as quickly. The gun fired and Jake's boot connected with the guilty fingers simultaneously. Blast deflected. Null safe. The holographic rabbit who'd come out to see what all the fuss was about wasn't so lucky.

Jake's follow-up combination removed the grey-haired inmate from the fray. He turned to Null. 'Wouldn't have hurt you to move, man.' The terrorist simply smiled enigmatically, like he'd known he was never in any real danger.

Like he didn't think he could be harmed.

Then the security officers had reached them and Null and Dark and Jake himself were being bundled out of the exercise chamber. 'All right, all right! I'm going!' he protested. He called them a few choice names, too. Had to live up to his cover story, didn't he? And speaking of which, surely saving the man's life had been sufficient to notify Null of his existence? The assassination attempt could hardly have come at a better time.

With or without Dark's help, Jake Black was on his way.

'I hope they won't mind,' said Lori.

'Who?' said Bex.

'Filders and Ross, of course, who else? Our fellow graduate agents whose entry codes we've just used – without their knowledge or permission – to get *in* here.'

Here was a Deveraux safe-house in Lexburg, Tennessee. As nothing of note ever seemed to happen in Lexburg, Tennessee, the organisation had not seen fit to maintain a tech in residence. Lori and Bex were alone, which suited their present purpose perfectly. Here more specifically was the safe-house's communications centre, complete with batteries of computers, IGC link, holocom projection capability and a cyber-cradle.

Deveraux's daughter paused as she brought the latter's systems on-line to cast her friend a lightly accusing stare. 'So who elected you the ethical half of the dynamic duo, huh, Lori? Ms *Angel*. Particularly as it was you who knew Filders and Ross' entry codes in the first place. I just keyed 'em in.'

'Cally's the one who's really responsible,' Lori corrected. 'She was the one who hacked into their files back at Spy High that time to prove the system needed updating. I was a witness, that's all.'

'Who just happens to have remembered the numbers two years later.'

'I'm good with numbers. I think it comes from boys keeping giving me theirs.'

'Well don't knock it.' Bex returned to her work. 'And if it'll salve that hypersensitive Angel conscience, we can apologise to Filders and Ross for taking their codes in vain when all this is over. But we didn't want to be checking in here under our own names, did we? Not with what I'm about to try.'

'You're right,' said Lori. Hacking into a fellow agent's files was one thing. Virtually infiltrating the private records of Jonathan Deveraux himself was something else entirely. 'This goes wrong,' she observed, 'and there'll be two more candidates for mind-wiping. For *real*.'

'Chill, Lo,' said Bex. 'Nothing's gonna *go* wrong.' With a hiss, almost of disapproval, the glass shield of the cyber-cradle lifted. 'Snow White's coffin awaits.' She kicked off her shoes. 'I've engaged the stealth capacity, so any security Dad's got on his files shouldn't even notice me, let alone recognise me. I've scrambled my cyber-signature as well, though. Guess we can't be too careful.'

'No,' Lori said significantly. 'We can't. You sure you don't want me to go in, Bex?'

She shook her blue-haired head emphatically. 'Thanks, Lo, but he's my dad – kind of. I feel responsible. It's got to be me.'

'Okay,' Lori consented, 'but who's being ethical now?'

'It's you, Angel. You're a bad influence. Now I'm cradling up before I start thinking I'll look good as a blonde.' Bex stepped into the cyber-cradle as if it was a shallow bath, lay back against the leather cushioning, strapped herself in. As the belt fastened, the glass shield began to lower, the virtual sensors to extend from the circuitry at the cradle's head in search of her temples. 'Don't go away, will you, Lo?' she said, more nervously than she'd intended.

She felt the sensors nuzzling against her skin like metallic pets in need of affection.

'I'll be right here,' Lori smiled reassuringly. 'I'll be keeping watch, Bex, don't worry. Anything happens, I'll over-ride and get you out manually.'

'My guardian Angel,' Bex said.

The cyber-cradle's shield clicked into place. There was a humming and a brief darkness as Bex closed her eyes.

Then, so much for friendship and loyalty. Lori was suddenly nowhere to be seen. Neither, incidentally, was the safe-house. Or any trace of Lexburg, Tennessee.

Bex appeared to be standing in the corridor at Spy High outside her father's quarters. She appeared to be wearing a glisteningly silver Deveraux shock-suit. But appearances were deceptive, in espionage more than most other occupations. Her flesh-and-blood body had not even twitched, was still reclining peacefully in its cyber-cradle under Lori's vigilant eye. Only her consciousness, digitalised and uploaded directly into the Spy High information network, had seemingly returned to school, and then only because she'd pre-set the coordinates for this place. Unless a specific costume was pre-selected, virtual agents always wore shock-suits, as if cyber-space was too prudish to permit nudity, and the familiar corridor, the door she'd opened many times before, they were the Deveraux system kindly providing its user with visual representations in three dimensions in order to avoid disorientation.

Bex was duly grateful to the system. It meant she could begin work immediately. She touched the door to her father's rooms and the oak panelling misted over before resolidifying into a computer keyboard and screen. There were not in reality rooms on the other side of the door, the barrier, but files, private files, and to access those you didn't knock. You hacked. Bex was not a computer natural like Cally, but she had flair, she'd been trained well, she was motivated and she had one advantage denied even to Cally. She was Mr Deveraux's daughter.

The keyboard and screen disappeared. The door was back. The door was opening.

She was in.

And the system was going to have to work harder in the avoiding disorientation stakes. Stepping through the doorway Bex entered what appeared to be a library, but it was a library that seemed liable to drive even the most ardent bibliophile biblio*phobic*. Shelves stretched higher than the eye could see, and lower too, an abyss yawning dizzyingly beneath her feet, and ahead of her the same endless ranks of silver spines placed on shelving of some gleaming, transparent substance. The floor on which Bex swayed, uncertain of her balance, seemed made from the same glass-like material. Her heart sank further than she could fall, which was a considerable distance. These weren't books stored here, of course; they were her father's files. And of the millions massed around her, she sought only one.

Maybe she should have given this job to Lori after all.

But no. Lori wouldn't have panicked, wouldn't have felt crushed and belittled by the scale of the place, wouldn't have felt the fear or the urge to retreat back into the corridor. Lori would have held her nerve and planned. Bex could do that. A journey of a thousand miles begins with but a single step. Some dead Chinese guy had said that. He was right. She needed to calm down and take one thing at a time.

Narrow her search. The files here were information. In cyber-space, *she* was essentially information. She could maybe interface with the library simply by *thinking* of what she wanted, creating a kind of file-link. *Jake Daly*, Bex concentrated. *Jake. Daly.*

She couldn't help it. She screamed as the floor was suddenly notable by its absence and she was plunging, plummeting, flailing her limbs crazily, the file shelves racing past her, the corridor lost on unreachable heights. She was like Alice tumbling down a very high-tech rabbit-hole, and if this bright chasm ever ended in something solid, Bex was going to be splattered all over it.

Except that when her descent was concluded, it was done politely, discreetly, even gently. There was floor again. She was standing. She began to wonder if she'd ever fallen. Where she was now appeared identical to where she'd been. Only it wasn't. No sight of the corridor, for one. And the files at her fingertips, *Jake Daly* was inscribed on their spines. Dismayingly, there were plenty of them, but Bex supposed she had time to browse.

'Unlawful trespass. Intruder alert.'

On the other hand, she hoped her speed-reading was up to scratch.

Her father's voice had never sounded so robotic before, so divorced from human tone and inflection. It was strangely chilling, It kept repeating the same words: 'Unlawful trespass. Intruder alert.' Maybe vocabulary in cyber-space was limited. Or maybe Dad had only one thing on his mind. She shouldn't have screamed. She'd been *heard*.

Had to be quick now. She was the virus and there had to be some kind of anti-virus security program.

Narrow her search still further. *Jake Daly mind-wipe*, she projected, and was immediately whisked to the right. Not far, however, and on the same level.

Twin sources of light that hadn't been there before coruscated both above and below her, admittedly hundreds of shelves apart. Not good news, though, Bex suspected. From the light: 'Unlawful trespass. Intruder alert.'

Luckily, the system wasn't entirely her enemy. Of all the files apparently dedicated to Jake, only one was flashing, as if keen to draw her attention. Bex obliged. *Jake Daly: Jake Black*, the spine read.

She could have kissed it. She didn't know why Jake had been given a new code-name, but she knew that this was the information she'd been looking for.

The twin lights were gliding towards her and in actual fact they were no longer lights. Each had taken the form of a human head. Jonathan Deveraux's head, to be precise, both of them. Brilliance was now confined to the founder's eyes, from which powerful beams probed and prowled like searchlights. She'd be caught in them soon.

'Unlawful trespass. Intruder alert.'

Bex grabbed the file from the shelf. In her hand it was more like a solid silver bar than a book. On what she'd expected to be a front cover, a single key inlaid in the centre. A single instruction above it: Press to Download. Bex pressed, replaced the file smartly. Now, whatever happened to her, the truth about Jake was downloading to the computer systems at the safe-house via those of the cyber-cradle. They'd be in Lori's possession any moment. Just as, if she didn't do something, she'd be in her father's.

A searchlight speared between her shoulderblades. 'Unlawful trespass. Intruder discovered.'

She ran. It was the default position on any mission, irrespective of how many years an agent had been in training. When in doubt, you ran. Sometimes it worked.

Sometimes, such as when you were being pursued by matching heads of the founder of the Deveraux College through a labyrinthine silver and glass library of his personal files with no way out and nowhere to hide, it didn't.

Bex was trapped in the glare of the searchlights. The security was closing in. 'Intruder discovered. Identity as yet unknown.' That was something. The cyber-signature scrambler was holding up. But she doubted it would for much longer.

Jonathan Deveraux's head rose through the floor in front of her like a ghost. His searchlight eyes were blinding. Bex threw up her arms to protect her own vision. 'Stay where you are. Do not move.'

How could she? It was over for her. Or no. It couldn't be. She wouldn't allow it. Spy High agents didn't go in for tame surrender. She'd be playing into her father's hands that way. And she *was*, Bex suddenly realised. She already was. She was accepting the file library as reality, when in truth it was only virtual. How *could* it be real, oversized heads rising up through the floor? She could escape, of course she could. She only had to do what anybody did when they were losing in a computer game and didn't want to continue.

'Exit program,' she breathed.

And there was darkness, but only until she'd opened her eyes again to see the cyber-cradle's shield lifting and Lori standing by. Bex felt a sigh of relief was in order.

'Welcome back,' said the blonde girl grimly. 'Have I got news for you.'

The Jake Black file told them everything. It confirmed

that the mind-wipe had been faked, revealed why. The animate was acting the dutiful farmer's son while the real Jake was engaging in Black Ops with carte blanche to do whatever he liked for the cause, even kill. Certainly kill. Killing Sicarius was the *point*.

'And this is all Dad's idea?' Bex was not happy. 'Of course it is. Nothing happens under the auspices of the Deveraux organisation that doesn't have my dad's approval. Maybe he should think about changing the old Spy High statement of intent, don't you reckon, Lori? "Keeping the world safe for tomorrow" sounds so Boy Scout these days, doesn't it? What about "Authorising Agents for Assassinations"? Got a certain ring to it.'

'At least we know where Jake is,' said Lori, her blue eyes clouded with concern. 'At least we know he hasn't killed anyone yet.'

'Do we?' Bex retorted. 'Okay, Sicarius must still be in the land of the living or else it'd be in the file, but Deepwater One isn't exactly a hovertel. Who knows what Jake might have to do to survive in there, and now he's got licence to do anything.'

'That's why we've got to *get* to him, talk to him,' Lori urged, 'before he does something he'll regret. I'm worried for him, Bex.'

'I know.' Bex laced a comforting arm around her friend's shoulder.

'I told you Jake can be bleak, and if he gets too close to these terrorists ... Their mentality, I think it's like a disease. I think it can *infect* you. And I think if you stare into darkness for too long, darkness is all you see.' Lori shuddered. 'We have to save Jake from himself or we could lose him for ever.'

'We won't lose him,' said Bex.

'It'll mean acting expressly against Mr Deveraux's – your father's – wishes,' Lori reminded her.

'What's he gonna do?' Bex joked with bravado. 'Send me to bed early?'

The communicator in her mission belt bleeped. Bex paled. Lori knew what the signal meant too. The girls looked at each other uneasily.

'Seems I'm wanted back at Spy High,' said Bex.

She was waiting for him on the mess hall landing. He could scarcely restrain a grin.

'Dark,' he said.

'Denver,' she said.

In her case, it seemed she could hardly keep from scowling, but Jake's ego was typical of the teenage boy. Dark was only trying to cover up her true feelings. She *liked* him.

'I need a word,' she added.

'Did I hear a please in there somewhere?'

'Don't push your luck. *Alone*.'

Jake was with Bugby. 'You go ahead, Soren,' he said. 'I'll be there in a minute.'

Bugby slouched resentfully into the mess hall, glowering at Dark as he passed.

'What a creep,' she grimaced. 'Makes my skin crawl. And you have to share a cell with him?'

'Are you making me a better offer?'

Dark snorted. 'I'm not offering anything. I'm telling.

Null wants to see you.' Jake's concealed grin turned into something harder, colder. This was it. 'In his cell. Now.'

'You mean I have to miss mealtime?' Now that he was in, play it cool.

'Not if you want to turn Null down,' Dark said, 'but you only get to turn him down once. Your choice.'

No choice.

Bugby's jealous remarks about Null's influence in the prison were borne out as Jake was led to the man's cell. The solitaries were supposed to be just that, kept at a distance from the rest of the prison population, usually for their own protection due to the nature of their crimes. In the Bringer's case, however, solitary appeared to be a sign of special treatment. To begin with, considerable latitude seemed to have been granted Null regarding the definition of solitary itself. Several of his followers, including Shaven-Head, were with him in his cell when Jake arrived, and while a little intercell fraternisation was also tolerated elsewhere in the jail, the sexes were kept apart and there were strict rules on how many prisoners were permitted to congregate in any one lockup at any one time. Ditto with books from the Deepwater library. The usual allowance was three volumes per inmate: Null's cell had one wall lined with the things. It seemed that power talked wherever you were in the world, even at the bottom of the sea. And like it or not, Null had power.

'Denver,' he said. 'Jake Denver.' Sampling the name as if it was a food he'd not tasted before and which he was uncertain he liked. 'Dark tells me you have an interest in the Bringers of the Night.'

'Then she's telling you right, Mr Null, sir,' Jake said.

'*Null*.' The terrorist's eyes flashed like fire. 'Call me Null.' Jake nodded. 'You fight well, Jake Denver. Yesterday in the exercise chamber you performed a service for me while my loyal disciples simply stood by. Stood by, Orme, hmm?'

Shaven-Head hung that particular portion of his anatomy in shame. Null was being a little unfair on Orme, Jake thought. *None* of the Bringers had been doing very much standing by as soon as the attack had commenced, whether or not they should have spotted its advent sooner. And Jake wondered whether the terrorist realised he was almost certainly storing up problems for his potential new recruit. Making him the cause of public humiliation for Orme was not conducive to future friendly relations between them.

'Naturally, I was never in any real danger,' Null continued. 'My destiny is not to die here, either at the hands of an assassin or through the incompetence of my followers. My destiny is to advance the cause of the Bringers of the Night. My destiny is to serve the great Sicarius and to join with him in bringing the gift of darkness to the world.' He smiled, and it seemed to Jake that behind Null's pasty, average features there was a demon lurking that longed to be unleashed. 'And you believe this to be your destiny also, Jake Denver?'

'If you'll . . . show me the way, Null,' Jake ventured.

It was a response that evidently pleased the terrorist. 'You fight well, as I have noted,' he replied, 'and combat skills are always valued in an organisation such as ours. But violence for its own sake is purposeless.

Only violence in a cause has meaning. Do you understand, Jake Denver? Will you be a weapon wielded in our cause?'

'I will.'

'Then we must talk further.' He dismissed the others from the cell.

Jake took the opportunity to scan the spines of Null's books. He seemed to have no personal possessions as such; maybe there'd be some clues to the inner workings of his mind here. The titles were not what he'd have expected. *The Future of Quantum Physics*. *The Theory and Practice of Dimensional Engineering*. *Man and the Multiverse*. *New Dimensions in Science*. Several were the work of a Professor L.A. Seerborn. Whatever else he might be, Null was clearly no fool.

'You are admiring my books, Denver?'

Stupid, Jake cursed himself. *Slow*. But remember for future reference, the Bringer didn't miss much either. 'Not really,' he lied. 'I'm not much of a reader.'

'Indeed not,' reflected Null. 'A reader, someone who loves learning, would not have razed a library to the ground, as I understand you did. An impressive statement – I shall not sully the deed by calling it a crime – and one of which I know the great Sicarius would approve, as I do. The increase of knowledge among Mankind has increased only sorrow, and the light that some claim it provides is but the weak, guttering flicker of a candle. The Bringers live to snuff it out, to cast Man back into the dark, secure dungeons of his ignorance. We would burn every book in the world if we could, every parchment, every page.'

Jake allowed his eyes to stray back to the tomes in Null's cell. This time he wanted the terrorist to notice.

'Yes, Denver,' he chuckled. 'Even those. Once they have served the greater good and outlived their usefulness. Destruction is the fate awaiting us all when our work is done.'

'Even Sicarius?' Jake dared.

'Oh, yes. Sicarius. Myself. Orme. Dark.' Null seemed to relish the prospect. 'Even you, Jake Denver.' He indicated that Jake should sit. 'Now, tell me what you already think you know about the Bringers of the Night.'

'Null? First? The attempt on your life yesterday, it seemed organised to me. Someone must have smuggled that shock blaster in . . .'

'Of course it was organised,' Null accepted with indifference. 'I have no doubt that it was sanctioned by the authorities. They fear us, you know, young Jake. They fear Sicarius. They will attempt any measure to thwart us in our purpose.'

'You think so?'

'But they will fail.'

'You think they'll try again? Here?'

'Perhaps. But I will tell you something, my young disciple, soon it will not matter.'

SIX

There were some advantages to being admitted into Null's inner circle, Jake supposed. The other cons tended to give him a wider berth now; a spare place always appeared for him in the mess hall, no matter how crowded it was. Even the guards seemed somehow to be granting him greater respect: nobody shouted at him any more. Jake wondered just how many of the security personnel could be trusted, and how many might not already be under Null's spell. Only Soren Bugby seemed unmoved by his young cellmate's elevation into the ranks of the Bringers. 'They never bring *me* nothing,' he growled. 'Think they're too good for the likes of me.' If anything, he seemed to resent the fact that in the exercise chamber Jake walked with new company.

Not that Jake cared about Soren Bugby. Not when he was now pretty much entitled to talk to Dark with impunity.

'So we're both Bringers of the Night now,' he said.

'Apparently.'

'So I think maybe we should get to know each other a little bit better.'

'Same old obsession,' Dark sighed. 'Are you sure you're one of us, Denver? Haven't you been listening to Null? *We* don't matter. *We're* as nothing. Only the cause counts, only the Night.'

'Is that why you call yourself Dark?' Jake probed. 'Kind of to get into the mood?'

'I told you before,' the girl asserted, 'Dark's my *name*. Besides, what does it really matter what we call ourselves? Or what we say about ourselves? It could all be lies. People lie all the time. Politicians lie. The media lies. Advids lie. Those pictures of perfect girls with perfect figures and perfect smiles, they lie. Cosmetics lie. Physical reconstruction lies. Society is built on falsehood.'

'Is that the truth?'

Dark uttered a sarcastic laugh, and for the first time Jake wondered whether there wasn't an ugliness in her after all. 'Take you, for example, and I wish someone would. Jake Denver. How do I know that's your real name? How do I know that if you told me your life story, and please don't even *think* about it, how do I know it wouldn't be a pattern of lies? Take *me* . . .'

'Is that a genuine offer or—'

'You want to know about me? I'm secretly a princess. I was the most beautiful princess ever born, so my father and mother the king and queen said, and I lived in a wonderful palace on a hill far away from the rest of the world where nobody could touch me. And I had a happy, smiling childhood in the wonderful palace, and when I grew up I was going to marry a prince. A *hand-some* prince, of course. And I could go anywhere I wanted to in the palace and do anything except one thing. I wasn't allowed to look out of the window in the topmost tower because anyone who did was cursed, my parents said, even beautiful princesses. Maybe especially beautiful princesses. And you know what? I tried and tried not to look, and I tried and tried to avoid going anywhere near the topmost tower, but in the end the temptation was too much. In the end I couldn't resist it any longer and I climbed the stairs and I pressed my face to the forbidden glass and I gazed out of the window. And I was *cursed*. I was cursed because what I saw was the real world, and it was filthy with lies and stinking with deceit and it was twisted and ugly and not beautiful at all. And I wanted to scream and run away and go back to being the princess playing out her happy, smiling childhood, but I couldn't. It was too late. The curse was on me. And because of it I was torn out of my princess' body and trapped in this one instead, and I was expelled from the wonderful palace and I came down from the hill to walk the world in exile. And I can never go back.'

There was a long silence.

'Did you make that up on the spot or is it a story you'd prepared beforehand?' said Jake.

The girl with the unfortunate hair and the protruding teeth fixed her cold green gaze on him. 'I want to forget my past. I want to forget everything. I don't want to think any more or be conscious. Consciousness is pain.

*Un*consciousness is peace. Sweet black oblivion. And that's what Sicarius and Null and the Bringers of the Night promise. That's why I'm one of them. *Peace*. Isn't that what everyone's looking for, Denver?'

Jake might have suggested that sponsoring atrocities such as the bombing of subway trains packed with innocent people was, in his opinion at least, a pretty warped way of finding peace. But then, he might have suggested a lot of things if his mission hadn't been to ingratiate himself with the Bringers in order to locate Sicarius. He had to suppress his true feelings for now. He had to keep them in the dark.

That was most difficult during his induction sessions with Null – his 'tutorials', as Sicarius' lieutenant liked to call them. Jake hadn't been aware that terrorists needed tutorials, but it seemed there was more to the work than a few pounds of gelignite concentrate and an utter contempt for human life.

Null explained it all. Bottom line: terrorists were teachers, and their victims a variation on the theme of the recalcitrant pupil who fails to learn his lesson.

Jake endured stolidly. He didn't actually have to pay too much attention to Null's rantings. His briefings before the commencement of his mission had told him all that was necessary for him to know about the Bringers of the Night. Mr Deveraux and Null just had different ideas as to their final judgement of Sicarius, that was all. Messiah or murderer. Jake knew which side he was on.

And what he was going to do about it.

'I only wish I could meet our great leader myself,' he professed humbly. 'It would be an inspiration.'

'Sicarius inspires by his words and by his deeds, Denver,' said Null. 'His presence is not important.' Jake adopted a suitably chastened expression. 'But I understand your feelings even so. Perhaps, one day, you and the leader might meet.'

'Not all the while we're stuck away in here, though,' Jake complained. 'I guess Sicarius is somewhere safe, isn't he? Somewhere the authorities won't find him.'

'The authorities will never apprehend Sicarius,' Null said with the certainty of the zealot.

Further, Jake urged himself. Now we're on the subject. Push him into giving a clue as to the maniac's whereabouts. If anyone knows, Null knows.

But it was Null who spoke first. 'And in any case, perhaps we will not always be incarcerated in Deepwater One.'

What? 'What do you mean, Null?'

The terrorist regarded the black-haired boy with amused superiority. 'You have learned much in a short time, Denver. I am pleased with you. If you wish to learn more, ensure that you are in the repair shop during work period tomorrow.'

'Sure, but why? Null, are we —'

'Our tutorial is ended, Denver. Remember what I have said.'

A breakout. It had to be. With either inside or outside help, Null was planning – *had* planned – an escape.

Which placed Jake in a dilemma. Did he go along with it, keep his cover, maybe risk involving himself with casualties among the security officers, who weren't simply going to stand by and wave the Bringers off to the surface? Or did he go to Connell, reveal his true identity and Null's intention, almost certainly saving lives but very definitely bringing his first Black Ops mission to an end and failure?

His options buzzed around his brain like wasps as he returned to his cell. Bugby was already there, sitting kind of scrunched up on his bunk and squeezing his knees like he wanted to burst them. 'You're back then?' Stater of the obvious.

'Looks like it, Soren.'

Jake leaned against the doorway, looking out on to the landing, the central shaft beyond it, an elevator flashing past to the levels below. Maybe his decision depended on how successful the escape attempt was likely to be. After all, if it worked, if Null got out, wouldn't he head straight for Sicarius?

'You've been with your new friends again, haven't you? Null and his kind.'

'Hmm? Looks like it, Soren.' His back was to Bugby.

'He thinks he's better than me, he does.' Squeezing, then punching his knees. 'I've seen him. I know.' Eyes like slits slashed by a switchblade. 'What about you, Denver?'

'What?' Relegating Bugby to background. Gauging whether it was actually possible to escape from Deepwater One. They'd need transport, of course. A sub. Did the Bringers' resources extend to submarines?

'You're not listening to me. You're not *listening*. I was wrong. Seems I was wrong. You're the same as the others after all.'

'Soren, what? Give it a rest, hey?' Maybe a better bet was the emergency evacuation subs. Which meant seizing the docking bay. Which meant seizing the control centre. Which was more heavily guarded than anywhere else. Which meant—

'You think you're better than me, don't you? *Admit it.*'

'What?' Bugby's tone was the warning.

'You think you're better than me, Denver. But you're *not*!'

Jake turned. His cellmate slammed into him like a runaway train. Half a second more of preparation and Jake could have rolled with Bugby's charge, thrown him to the concrete floor and ended this mismatch immediately. Trouble was, half a second was all he got, and even Deveraux training needed time to deploy.

Breath pounded from his lungs, Jake was lifted and carried by the savagery of Bugby's stampede. And his maddened cellmate wasn't stopping. He was driving on.

The landing wasn't actually that wide. The guardrail protecting the cons from a vertical drop of over a hundred metres wasn't actually that high.

Jake got to thinking that Bugby's trajectory was not accidental.

He chopped hard at the older man's ears. Bugby cried out in pain, faltered, instinctively raised his hands to his head. Let go of Jake.

Now he could make use of gravity and concrete.

But Bugby was either too stupid or too incensed to stay down. 'Think you're a better . . . fighter than me.' Groping to his feet.

'Soren,' sighed Jake, assuming a defensive posture, 'you need major therapy, you know that?'

Bugby lunged. Jake sidestepped, struck clinically at the nerve centres to temporarily paralyse his adversary's right arm. Maybe that was the wrong move. Now he felt bad about having to hit a one-armed man.

Other prisoners spilling from their cells, cheering not Jake, not Bugby, cheering the fight. Guards sprinting along the landing to put an end to it.

Jake did that himself, a blow to Bugby's stomach doubling him up and sinking the crim to his already battered knees.

'. . . better than . . . urgh . . .'

'I guess this means you want me to move out,' said Jake. 'It's okay, guys. It's all over. Sorry for the disturbance.' To the guards who seized his arms and dragged him towards the landing's command point. Soren Bugby was being hauled up also. An awful possibility occurred to Jake. 'Ah, officers, where are we going?'

'You and Bugby seem a little hot-tempered,' grinned a guard humourlessly. 'A few days in the punishment cells should cool you down.'

Fathers and daughters, thought Rebecca 'Bex' Deveraux. She knew the relationship between them could be fraught with tension and friction. The former reluctant to let their little girls grow up; the latter keen to rebel to prove they already had. Fathers and *teenage* daughters, in need of a professional negotiating team to help them get along most of the time. So she understood. So she read.

Personally, of course, she hadn't always had a lot of experience with the father–daughter thing. Example: bringing the first boyfriend home to meet the folks, to meet Dad, who probably suspected that First Boyfriend was only after One Thing. A rite of passage if ever there was one. Bex had never done it, brought the boyfriend home to meet the folks, not her first boyfriend, not her second, who was in any case only weeks behind her first, not any of them. And even if there were any candidates for the post left, it was a trend she could see continuing. Largely because her mother was dead – terminally – and her father was dead but evidently hadn't liked it and had come back as a computer program with, at the moment, as she stood between them in his rooms at Spy High, twelve digital heads, one for each ceiling-suspended screen.

Fathers and daughters, thought Rebecca 'Bex' Deveraux. They sometimes got to hug each other too. And sometimes a daughter could go crying to Dad and he'd make everything all right. So she understood. So she read.

If only.

'You wanted to see me, Dad?' She was allowed to be informal when none of her fellow operatives was present.

'Something has come to my attention, Rebecca.' Ditto the computerised man.

And it must be easy for him to remain inscrutable, Bex reasoned, to preserve an expression that gave nothing away. It was merely a matter of playing with pixels. Was he doing that now? His image was as aloof and impassive as ever, but what was he really *thinking*? Did he suspect it had been his own daughter intruding among his private files? The summons coming when it had couldn't have been coincidence. Did he *know*?

And if he did, was he mad?

'I understand you have requested a fortnight's leave of absence.' She had indeed. 'Is there any particular reason for this?'

To save Jake from this Black Ops nightmare you've railroaded him into. The words in Bex's mind. 'No. Nothing in particular.' The words on her lips.

And while it might be easy for a computer to betray no emotion, it was more difficult for her. She was still human. Difficult, but essential. She must reveal *nothing*. Her training would help. And there was always the example of her father to follow.

'I ask because this is the first time that you have made such a request,' said Deveraux. 'It seems out of character for you, Rebecca. Is anything wrong?'

'No.' Accompanied by a little how-could-there-be laugh. 'Of course not.'

'The mind-wiping of Agent Daly does not trouble you?'

Bex wondered if she was starting to sweat. If she was, she wondered whether the sensors in her father's rooms would detect it and deduce the reason why. Best not to offer a *total* lie at this point. 'Sure, what happened to Jake bothers me,' she admitted. 'We were partners, friends. That's natural, isn't it? But I understand why he was mind-wiped. I'll get over it.'

'If there was anything worrying you, you would come to me, would you not?' the computerised man probed. 'As your superior, Rebecca. As your father.'

'Of course I would.' No alternative but the total lie to that one.

'An organisation such as ours,' Deveraux said, 'we must remain eternally vigilant. Despite our best efforts, the world beyond these walls is still a dangerous and a treacherous place, perhaps these days more so than ever. It seems incredible, but there has even been a recent breach of security here, at Deveraux itself.'

Bex hoped her eyes appeared wide with shock rather than guilt. 'Really?'

'The integrity of my private files was briefly compromised.'

'Do you know who by? I mean, did you track them down?'

'Unfortunately not, but clearly the trespasser was either a highly proficient computer hacker or someone with access to Deveraux technology. Or both.'

A single pair of her father's unblinking eyes boring into her own would have been unsettling enough. Twelve of them was almost unbearable. The slightest twitch of a muscle or quaver in her voice could give her away. 'Do you know which files they were after? That'd be a clue, maybe.'

He did know. He *must* know. Fathers knew everything. He was toying with her, giving her a chance to confess voluntarily before revealing the truth himself. It was tempting. Bex was tempted. And sometime a daughter could go crying to her dad and he'd make everything all right. But she had loyalties. To Lori. To Jake.

And her father was saying: 'It is impossible to identify which files the intruder sought, and in any case it seems his presence was detected before damage could be done. Even so, new security measures are now in place. Such an incident will not occur again.'

'That's good, Dad.' He *didn't* know. He might suspect, but there was no evidence. Bex and Lori were still in the game. 'My leave?'

'Granted,' said Jonathan Deveraux. 'Of course.'

Bex walked steadily, even slowly, out of her father's rooms.

Then she kicked up her heels and ran.

Of all days, Jake cursed inwardly. Of all the days for Bugby to lose it and get them both thrown into the punishment cells. It had to be the day before Null's breakout attempt. So now here he was, a dozen levels below the repair shop, and the number of hours between the present moment and the time he needed to be *in* the repair shop rapidly diminishing. At least he no longer had to share his cell with Bugby or, indeed, anyone else.

And at least his predicament had clarified his course of action. No chance now of joining Null's escape and reaching Sicarius that way. Therefore, the Bringers could not be allowed to leave the prison at all.

Only one thing for him to do.

'Listen, this is important. It's *vital* I speak with Chief Officer Connell.'

Initially, the guards on the punishment level were not impressed. 'Change the record, Denver. How many times have we told you? Chief Officer Connell won't want to talk to *you*.'

'He will when he hears what I've got to say. Fetch him. *Do* it. Your lives and the lives of everyone in this prison could be at stake.'

They wanted to scoff, the security officers, they wanted to ignore the Denver kid with the big mouth and the piercing eyes, but there was something about him, an authority, a relentlessness, a kind of truth, that as time wore on and night became morning made them wonder. It couldn't do any harm to contact Chief Officer Connell, could it? And what if the kid *did* somehow know something significant? He hung around with Null and those creepy Bringers of the Night, didn't he?

'Chief Officer Connell will be down to see you today, Denver,' Jake was finally informed. '*When* he can find the time.'

With work period almost upon them – prisoners in the punishment cells excluded, of course – time was a commodity in short supply.

'Not good enough!' Jake protested. 'He's got to come now. It's Null. Tell him it's to do with Null.'

Maybe he should have disclosed more information to the guards sooner, but he wasn't sure how far they could be trusted. Connell was a safer bet. In mission situations, you confided in non-Deveraux personnel only as a last resort and at the last minute. For Jake, both seemed to have arrived.

Null's name must have done the trick. The Chief Security Officer appeared at his door within minutes, flanked by both of the punishment level's two resident guards. All three men entered Jake's cell.

'You're getting loud again, Denver,' Connell said disapprovingly. 'You're making noise that I'm hearing all the way up in my private office.'

'Chief Officer Connell,' Jake said, 'you've got to sound the general alarm. Null and his followers are planning an escape and it's set for work period today. You can still stop it if you move quickly.'

Connell's eyebrows rose in apparent astonishment.

'Didn't you hear me? They're gonna break out. *Now.* Work period's about to start.'

The two guards glanced at their superior officer to gauge the response they should take to Denver's revelation. It seemed to be sceptical.

'On what grounds do you base this wild claim?' Connell asked coolly.

'Null told me. Said I needed to be in the repair shop for work period today.' Why wasn't Connell *doing* anything? 'They'll be in the repair shop. Maybe they've got weapons hidden there or something.'

'Unlikely,' judged Connell. 'How could even Null procure weapons in Deepwater One?'

'Who cares? Maybe he had inside help. Maybe one of your guards . . .'

'Are you questioning the integrity of my staff?' Chief Officer Connell demanded.

'Look, Connell' – Jake could hardly contain his frustration – 'just check it out. The repair shop. You're wasting time.'

'I feel I'm wasting time attending to the intemperate

rantings of a criminal who is, after all,' Connell pointed out, as if he deserved credit for doing so, 'one of this man Null's known associates. What kind of ruse are you trying to pull, Denver?'

The Chief Security Officer's self-satisfied smile was echoed by his minions.

'My name's not Denver,' said Jake. No time meant no choice. Deepwater One was a dead end. Best to cut his losses and start again. 'I'm not a criminal, either. I'm working undercover for an organisation involved in counterterrorist operations.'

'Is that so?' said Connell, attentively, as if at last he was believing the prisoner and realising the gravity of the situation.

'My mission was to infiltrate the Bringers of the Night.'

'That does place a rather different complexion on matters, does it not? Let me think . . .' Connell turned away contemplatively. The two guards dutifully kept their eyes on Jake.

'Don't you believe me?' the teenager pressed.

'Of course I believe you,' said Connell, 'otherwise I wouldn't be doing *this* . . .'

He turned again. He'd drawn his shock blaster. He shot one guard with it. The second instinctively reached for his own. So Chief Security Officer Connell shot him, too.

Before Jake could react, the gun was pointing squarely at his chest.

'Looks like you're next, then,' said Connell.

SEVEN

'Taking out your own men, Chief Officer,' tutted Jake. 'Looks like you work in the right place.'

'Well you're in the *wrong* place, Denver, or whatever your name is,' retorted Connell, 'and you're going to regret it. Hands. Where I can see them.'

Jake raised his hands but his muscles were tensed for action. He'd been held at gunpoint before. No doubt he would be again. Occupational hazard for a secret agent.

'And to correct you,' the older man continued, 'it was not *I* who murdered Frederic and McGuire – it was *you* during your reckless attempt to escape. It just so happened that I was close by to put an end to your rampage and, sadly but unavoidably, your life.'

'You should have written fiction for a living, Connell,' Jake said. 'You'd have been a wow. So how much is Null paying you to betray your trust?'

'Payment?' Connell chuckled. 'Nothing in monetary terms. He *persuaded* me, Denver. He made me a promise.'

'What? A seat on the right hand of Sicarius?'

Connell shook his head. 'Silence,' he claimed. 'That's what I've been promised. In the darkness that the Bringers will gift to the world there is only silence. Null told me so. He pledged it to me. And it's what I want. Quietness. Peace. There's too much *noise* . . .'

As if to prove the Chief Officer's point, a hollow boom sounded from somewhere higher in the prison. A sound that Jake for one registered with apprehension. The building, too. It shuddered.

'Sounds like work period's going with a bang,' Jake observed. 'Your new friends want out.'

'Impossible. Now isn't the time. Null told me it would be tomorrow.' A second explosion shook Deepwater One, muffled by distance, then a third. Shouts of alarm from the punishment level's other guests. 'I've been betrayed!' Connell, rather unprofessionally, glanced upwards.

Jake, entirely professionally, connected his boot to the man's chin. 'If you're expecting sympathy, forget it!' As Connell staggered back against the wall of the cell, Jake struck out again, disarmed him, rammed his hip into him and threw. 'My pa always used to say, if you do business with a cheat, expect to be cheated. Hey, guess who's got the blaster now?'

Connell was sprawling on the floor. He didn't seem to care. 'Shoot me, then. I'd sooner be shot than drown. One last noise and then silence.'

'Think I'd prefer Option C: neither of the above. Drown? Explain.'

'Isn't it obvious?' Connell burst into a laughter that could have been crying. 'What kind of undercover agent are you?'

'One that's still got a job to do.' Jake hauled Connell up by his collar. 'On your feet, Chief Officer, sir.'

Because it *was* obvious. Explosions in an edifice under the sea, reinforced walls of concrete and steel the sole barrier between those within and the greedy, inundating waters without. Blow a hole in those walls with gelignite concentrate, no doubt supplied by a certain traitor in a uniform not too far away, and like any uninvited guest on the surface, the ocean'll come calling and make itself at home.

A diversion of major proportions while Null and co. stormed the control centre.

Jake shoved Connell ahead of him towards the punishment level's command point. The semicircular suite of computers curved in front of the central elevators.

The general alarm was already jangling. Difficult to hear much from the levels above with the crims incarcerated here howling in growing panic, but wasn't that pulse rifle fire?

'Is Null armed?' Jake demanded.

'Yes, yes, of *course* he's armed. Rifles, blasters, stashed in the repair shop. I saw to it myself.' Connell was aggrieved. 'But the escape was planned for *tomorrow*.'

And what was that, splattering against Jake's cheek, wetting his black hair? It felt like the first drops of rain before a downpour. But it wasn't rain. It was much, much worse than rain.

If the prisoners were in tumult now, they were going to be in a total frenzy soon.

Jake had been trained in the operation of Deepwater's hardware, just in case. He forced Connell into a chair, kept the blaster trained on him while with his other hand he worked the computers.

'What are you doing? What are you *doing*?'

'First thing, I'm engaging the central cell release mechanism. Nobody's gonna go blub-blub-blub without a chance of saving themselves if *I* have anything to do with it.'

Connell blanched in horror. 'You're letting this scum out? They'll tear us apart!'

'*You*, maybe,' corrected Jake. 'Not me. Because *second* thing, I'm programming the elevator that brought you down to take me up to the recreation level. Express service. No stops. I'm already late for my appointment with Null.'

Doors slid open throughout the punishment level.

'You can't do this!' Connell protested desperately. 'Denver, you can't leave me here. Not with them!'

Cons already swarming from their cells. None of them too happy.

'You like silence so much, Connell,' remarked Jake, 'try and preserve some. Maybe the crims won't notice you.'

He dared not delay any longer, not if he still intended to salvage his mission. He darted into the elevator and pressed the button for the recreation level. The computer would ensure that he'd reach it without interruption. The doors closed on a wailing Chief Officer Connell.

By the time he'd ascended a single level Jake had thrust Null's puppet to the back of his mind. He was thinking ahead, shaping his story. Null must have been aware he'd been placed in the punishment cells so half of it was true in any case. He'd escaped and had made his way directly to join his fellow Bringers. They'd welcome him as an ally. They'd *need* him if there was still fighting to be done, which seemed likely. He didn't have to mention the confrontation with Connell. It seemed Null had always planned on leaving the security man behind anyway.

The cell levels flashed past. Jake's expression became grim. He was nearing the site of the explosions and the charges responsible for them had clearly been expertly placed. Water was cascading into the prison as if from unseen cataracts, crashing in huge spouts of spray from one landing to the next below, gushing over guardrails, surging like a young Niagara into the deep well of the penitentiary's central shaft, and deep it might be, but as the remorseless pressure of the ocean outside widened the wounds in the walls inflicted by Null's gelignite concentrate, as ever-greater volumes of water forced their way in like a swirling, surrounding mob, sooner or later the deluge would make its mark. First the punishment cells would be flooded, then the cells on the level immediately above, then those above *them*. The process was already underway. It couldn't be stopped.

Deepwater One was drowning.

Its human inhabitants didn't have to be told. The clamour and the chaos on every level was proof they already knew precisely what was happening. Jake saw guards trying to evacuate those prisoners still in their cells. If everyone was following procedure, they'd quickly be reinforced either by off-duty colleagues or those normally engaged in administrative tasks. They'd

need to be. The fact that the guards were now attempt-
ing to save their lives did not in the convicts' minds
compensate for the uniforms they wore and the perceived repression they'd enforced in the past. There
were struggles. There was gunfire. There was a word
for it that every employee within the penal system
dreaded hearing: *riot*. And most of the inmates were at
their work period locations, not on their cell landings at
all. What was the mood going to be like where Jake was
heading?

The elevator smoothed to a stop. He'd know in the
time it took for the doors to open.

It was as well they operated without reference to
external events. If they'd parted more quickly, as the
teenager was urging them to do, the pulse rifle blast
would have drilled him to the back wall and put a pre-
mature end to Jake Black's career. As it was, only the
steel of the elevator door suffered, and that preserved a
stoical silence.

So discipline and order had collapsed throughout the
jail. Basically, it was every man for himself. The situation
was playing perfectly into Null's hands.

Jake had to find him.

He bolted from the elevator, keeping low, shock
blaster wary. There was carnage on the recreation
landing, pitched battles between crims and guards, but
to even attain the landing he had to negotiate the thin
ribbon of bridge that connected it to the elevator. No
Deveraux agent was allowed the luxury of acrophobia
or even aquaphobia, but the combination of dizzying
height and the deep drop below torrenting with water

wasn't designed to boost anyone's confidence. The bridge suddenly seemed to Jake as frail and brittle as an old man's backbone. He also realised that he was in danger not so much from the convicts as from the prison guards.

A shock blast struck the bridge's handrail. Jake instinctively returned fire. Case in point: he'd just felled one of the Good Guys. Luckily, his own blaster was on Stun. Jake did not plan on slaughtering his way to Sicarius.

But he was a sitting duck on the bridge. He raced for the landing. Shock blasts sparked the steel at his feet like firecrackers. He felt his boots singe. And then one burst of fire, closer still, pitching him sideways, his balance momentarily lost.

The handrail jabbed into his side, did its best to prop him up. It failed. Jake's momentum took him over the edge. All of a sudden he was in space. The watery chasm beckoned, and though a Deveraux agent could do many things to save himself from certain death in the field, flying wasn't one of them.

Lashing out with his arm, however, and seizing a handrail dozens of metres above the ground at the last possible second, that *was*. So was mustering the strength and discipline to hang there, limb racked and muscles on fire, until he could do something about it.

The guard taking potshots at him from the landing was preventing Jake from improving his position immediately. Had to change that. In his dangling right hand he still held his shock blaster. Firmly. He took out the guard with his first shot.

The clatter of boots on the bridge. Strong hands clasping his arm.

'What?' Jake looked up. Friend or foe?

For the moment, both.

'So pleased you could join us at last, Jake.' Null.

'What do you think you're doing there, Denver?' Dark.

'Me? I'm just hanging around.' Sometimes, the old lines were still the best.

'That will never do,' said Null. 'There is work to be done. *Up*, Jake Denver, and take your place with the Bringers of the Night.'

And Null hauled him up, Sicarius' loyal lieutenant, a murdering terrorist himself, had saved his life. Lori would have called it irony.

Jake called it a bummer.

'Now quickly, all of you, into the transportation our newest recruit has so thoughtfully provided.'

They were all on the bridge, Null's little clique of lunatics, all heavily armed.

'Guns courtesy of Chief Security Officer Connell,' Dark informed Jake as the group crammed into the elevator. Jake was shocked, a reaction the girl relished. 'Connell was with us, but we aren't with *him*. Null deceived him.'

'He deceived himself,' Null corrected, 'as all men do. Orme. The over-ride.' Shaven-Head handed his leader a small metal device that Null affixed to the elevator's control panel. Jake realised it performed the same function as the program he'd keyed in himself on the punishment level computers. The elevator was now the terrorists' private property. 'The control centre, I think. And thank you for saving us from having to summon this elevator ourselves, Jake. It and its partner are the only ones with access to where we want to go.'

'You broke out of the punishment cells then?' Dark seemed quite excited.

'Heard the explosions. Two and two. Couldn't let you leave without me.' Whether the *you* was intended to be plural referring to the Bringers as a whole, or singular, Dark only, neither Jake nor she seemed entirely certain. Safer for the secret agent to turn to Null. 'I assume we're going for the subs, but won't the controllers have already informed the surface what's happening?'

'They'll have tried.' Null produced a second metal object, this time adorned with flashing lights and this time from about his own person. 'A little gadget of mine. Emits a jamming signal. Quite powerful. The surface has not the faintest idea that Deepwater One is currently undergoing a rather radical change in its power structure.' The elevator reached the control centre. 'Let us now complete the process.'

The doors opened. The Bringers burst through them all guns blazing.

Including Jake's. What choice did he have? This was what it meant to be undercover, to be in Black Ops. You had to pretend you were of the same mind as the scumbags around you, you had to act the assassin, masquerade as the murderer. But at the same time, mired in the filth of their sickness and cruelty, you had to keep yourself sane, remember who you truly were, remember you were the Good Guy.

Don't lose yourself in the darkness.

So Jake rampaged through the control centre at Null's side because Null could get him to *Sicarius'* side, and he tried not to look at the terrified faces of the controllers gunned down at their consoles or blasted in the back as they fled as blindly as rabbits from the hunter, and he tried not to hear the shouts and the cries of the security officers left to guard the nerve centre of the prison while their colleagues were dispatched to the disturbances below, and the explosions and the screams and the shattering of screens, the eruptions of circuitry, the spilling of blood, Jake tried to shut all that out. He was like a man engulfed in flame who would sooner not get burned.

The deadly conversation of gunfire ceased, an argument which had finally proved unanswerable. Most of the Bringers still stood, Null, Orme and Dark included. None of the controllers.

'You've done well, Jake,' said Null admiringly. 'You have brought the blessing of night to many. You will indeed be an asset to our organisation.'

As long as nobody looked too closely at his apparent victims, Jake thought, because then they might see that the night his stun blasts had brought them was temporary. He only wished he could have cut down the entire control centre.

'You, on the other hand, Dark,' Null said critically, 'seem to have stumbled on your way. Did you bring the blessing of night to *anyone*?'

'My blaster,' Dark complained, 'it kept jamming. I'm sorry, Null.'

'It matters not. You will have other opportunities. Now . . .' He moved swiftly to one of the computers that was not damaged, brought life to the viewing screens that were not dead.

Jake watched Null closely. *Definitely* not to be under-estimated. These devices he'd knocked up, the speed with which he operated the computer now, it seemed that terrorists could be skilled at science as well as at slaughter. And his slight frame belied significant physical strength too: Null had lifted him at the bridge without strain. He was a dangerous man, maybe nearly as dangerous as Sicarius.

One of the viewing screens showed the docking bay adjacent to the control centre. A mere handful of guards seemed prepared to deny access to the emergency evacuation subs. 'Orme, eliminate resistance and secure our submarine,' Null ordered. Jake started to follow Orme. 'No. Jake. Guard my back while I finish my work here.'

Work? The rest of the screens displayed scenes from some of the lower levels. The punishment cells were now submerged. The sea was thundering in with greater impunity, like an army assured of victory, the walls of the prison crumbling little by little. Prisoner and guard alike seemed to have passed the stage of mindless conflict and were united in a common cause: survival.

Null was nearly misty-eyed at the sight. 'You see, Jake, how the prospect of night brings even sworn enemies together. What *good* we do the world.'

'Work?' said Jake.

There was gunfire again close by. The Bringers and

the guards disputing possession of the only way out of the flooding penitentiary.

'Indeed. Or pleasure. To me they are the same. We must ensure that nobody interferes with our escape or arrives to bolster the forces that still face us. Did you know there are emergency doors that seal off the control and docking levels from all those below, Jake?' Jake did, but he professed otherwise. 'I'm closing them now and disabling their manual operation systems. We shan't be interrupted.'

On the lower levels, impregnable steel barriers locked into place. Those trapped thereby pounded and bludgeoned them with their fists, fired futile shock blasts, widened their eyes in dawning horror.

'They'll all drown.' Jake's throat was dry.

'But we will not even get our feet wet. Come.' Null rose and moved in the direction of the docking bay. '*Denver.*'

'Yes, Null.' And he was obeying. He was leaving the control centre with the terrorist, leaving several hundred men and women to drown. Even the likes of Soren Bugby deserved a better fate than that. What could he do? How could he act without betraying who he was? But how could he *not* act? Betrayals came in many forms.

'It appears Orme has succeeded in his mission,' Null observed.

The Bringers, reduced in number to Orme, Dark and only two others, held the docking bay.

'You go on,' Jake suddenly urged his companion. 'I've got to go back. I . . . in the control centre . . .'

'What?' Null's eyes flashed.

'I . . . saw somebody moving. A guard. I'm sure of it.'
Jake was backing away, ready to take Null out if the terrorist chose not to believe him. 'He's still alive.'

'Then rectify the matter,' dictated Null.

Jake sprinted back into the ruined control centre. Lucky, *lucky*. The screens showed the water levels rising, the emergency doors unbreachable. He fired his blaster to cover his true purpose. He was at *least* as good on a keyboard as any cold-hearted, murdering scumbag. The emergency doors were no longer going to be a problem. The population of Deepwater One would be able to evacuate in the other subs.

Jake just hoped he and Null's group were gone before they reached the docking bay.

He hurtled to the sub. Dark was at the hatch yelling for him to hurry. The magnetic core was already energised. Null was wasting no time, which suited him just fine.

Jake spilled aboard.

And their leader could operate a submarine, too. There was no end to his talents. 'Did you resolve our little problem satisfactorily?' he wanted to know.

'Didn't even get my feet wet,' Jake said.

Sicarius, he was thinking darkly, here I come.

At first, Soren Bugby hadn't intended to cooperate. Why should he? The screws had very nearly let him drown, and they'd *always* thought they were better than him, looking at him down their noses in their crisp new uniforms. But then he took a look at the two who wanted to interview him about Denver. If *all* the screws carried off their crisp new uniforms like this pair, he might very well end up a reformed character.

'Ask away, girls,' he said generously. 'Whatever you like. You'll find me very helpful.'

The one with the nose stud and the dyed black hair said she'd sooner not have found a sleaze like him at all, which he didn't think was too friendly, but the blonde put her in her place and told him they really really appreciated his assistance really. He preferred the blonde anyway. A little piece of Heaven she looked like, though ordinarily Bugby hated the idea of Heaven. Loads of dead guys who thought they were better than you 'cause they had Saint in front of their names. He wondered if the blonde and her friend would be interested in his views on such matters, but the one with the nose stud and the dyed black hair said the only views she was interested in were those without him in the foreground, and even the blonde said she'd sooner just talk about Denver.

So they did. He told them everything he knew. Yes, he and Denver had been sent to the punishment cells together, but it was the kid's fault, he thought he was *better* than . . . Yes, Denver had been hanging around with Null and his lunatic Bringers of the Night, had got his feet *right* under the table as far as that went. No, he hadn't seen the kid during the escape, not personally, though a fellow con called Michaels who'd been in the punishment cells too had sworn to him that it was Denver who'd let them out. (No, he hadn't done *that* to Chief Officer Connell, and was he likely to regain consciousness any time soon?) No, he wouldn't be surprised if Denver had left with Null. If he wasn't in the Transfer Centre holding tanks with the rest of them and if his body hadn't been recovered like the other fatalities, where else could he have gone?

The blonde and her friend with the nose stud sighed, sighed like they'd known that all along, sighed like it was personal. Then they thanked him – or at least the blonde did – and left.

It was strange, though. When a couple more screws, the usual type this time, came to ask for a statement, and when he complained that he'd already given one, they stared at him blankly. Even when he described the blonde and her friend with the nose stud. Even when he *insisted*, insisted to the point of violence. They had him sent for medical examination. Medtechs proved Soren Bugby was suffering from wish-fulfilment fantasies brought on as a side-effect of post-traumatic stress disorder.

Nobody answering the descriptions he'd given was employed by the prison authorities.

Jake peered out from the helicopter. Bleak, brooding mountains and steep-sided, inhospitable valleys. Nothing growing and no sign of human settlement. Not exactly package tour country. But then the remote and danger-ous territory straddling the border between Pakistan and Afghanistan had never been popular with anyone but warlords, terrorists and the occasional wayward goat-herder. This was where Null had brought them; at least it was Jake's best bet for a location. There weren't any signposts, but a Deveraux agent's sense of geography was trained to be acute. And wherever it was, it was where he wanted to be. When they landed, they would meet Sicarius.

Jake glanced across at his companions, Null, Orme, Dark and the two other survivors from the breakout at Deepwater One. Null's talents did not, it seemed, extend to flying a helicopter – a pilot and co-pilot were doing that – or maybe he just didn't want to show off. Dark saw Jake looking, averted her gaze. She'd done a lot of averting since they'd left the sub and taken to the air. Perhaps things would change once they were on the ground again.

Which was going to be soon. Jake felt his heart thudding harder as the pilot began his descent. To where, though? The valley beneath them now resembled twin lips sworn to secrecy. No way he could take the chopper down there, surely.

The pilot knew the terrain better than Jake, which was just as well for all of them. The helicopter skimmed the ridge until suddenly the valley widened, not by much, not for long, but sufficiently on both counts to permit entrance.

There were buildings below, hugging the valley walls as if afraid of the wider world. The home base of the Bringers of the Night.

Jake realised his hand was resting on the butt of his shock blaster.

They were greeted warmly by their fellow Bringers, a motley collection of nationalities and ethnic types some two dozen strong. Hardly an army, but it only took one

fanatic with a death-wish to commit an atrocity. Jake
had wondered whether Sicarius himself might not lead
the welcome party, embrace his returning lieutenant and
applaud his loyal soldiers.

They had to make do with someone called Dravic, a
man with so many sharp edges to his features that if he
ever scratched his stubbled chin he probably risked
cutting himself. His eyes were like blades, glittering as if
they could slice through a man's masks and pretences to
expose the truth beneath. Jake knew he'd need to be
wary of Dravic.

'It is good to see you again, brother,' the sharp-edged
man laughed with Null, 'but what kept you? We were
beginning to think you had gone into voluntary retire-
ment.'

Null seemed to consider such a prospect unlikely. 'Our
new recruits.' He introduced Jake and Dark. 'Both
have already proven themselves strong in the cause.
They are keen to meet with Sicarius.'

'Are they?' Dravic's good humour continued unde-
terred. 'Of *course* they are. Then meet with Sicarius they
must. Follow me, Denver, Dark.'

Dravic led them through the complex, Null accompa-
nying. Orme and the others had already dispersed with
their Bringer comrades. The teenagers' route took them
deep into the rock of the valley wall itself, through
tunnels and chambers hollowed out over time, easy to
defend and therefore difficult to capture in any assault.
Lighting was minimal.

The great Sicarius, Jake thought derisively, cowering
underground like a frightened animal, like a living man

in a grave. But not to worry, Sicarius. Jake Black was coming to put you out of your misery.

Finally they entered a cavern curiously lit from below. Computers and other high-tech instrumentation huddled in the shadows as if believing it was better not to be noticed. Dravic crossed to a console.

'This is where Sicarius makes those broadcasts he feels are appropriate to bring the cause of night to the attention of a doubting world.' Null ushered the youngsters forward. 'Please. Our great leader is waiting for you.'

Jake moved uncertainly towards the middle of the chamber, Dark close beside him, almost touching. 'So where is he? I thought you said we could meet Sicarius?'

'Sicarius is with you,' said Null.

And he was. Suddenly, shockingly, he was. Garbed in long, flowing robes. His wild mane of hair black as pitch. His eyes blazing with dark fire as they transfixed the two teenagers. His teeth bared in arrogant contempt.

His feet not touching the ground.

'Sicarius?' Dark's voice was almost a whisper.

'It can't be,' Jake breathed. 'I don't believe it.' But then he put out his hand and it went through Sicarius and he had no choice but to believe it. 'A hologram. He's a *hologram*.'

'Indeed,' said Null, advancing. Dravic was laughing from the computer console in the manner of a trickster whose prank had gone well. 'A hologram. Every feature, every mannerism, every inflection of the voice researched and then computer-generated to strike maximum fear into the hearts of those who profess to believe in light. The realisation of their deepest dread. The *ultimate* terrorist.'

'I don't understand.' Dark was struggling. 'Do you mean there *is* no Sicarius? That this is all a deceit?'

'You are looking on the public face of our organisation, Dark, nothing more.'

'So Sicarius doesn't actually exist?'

'Of course he exists.'

'Then where is he, Null?' Jake joined his voice to the girl's.

'Haven't you guessed?' Null echoed Dravic's laughter and opened his arms modestly. '*I* am Sicarius.'

EIGHT

He was an idiot, Jake cursed inwardly. A fool. He deserved to be mind-wiped for real.

His mission was to locate and put an end to Sicarius. Instead, he'd unwittingly helped the terrorist escape from custody and return to a freedom he was unlikely to use to open a charity shop. If he'd only *known*, he could have acted in the prison, arranged an accident during one of his tutorials with 'Null', maybe, or allowed the assassination attempt in the exercise chamber to take its course.

If he'd only known . . .

'*Null*,' said Sicarius. 'From the Latin word *nullus*, meaning none. A clue to the fact that I was not who I appeared to be, had the ignorant clods in the so-called security services the education to recognise it. And you want to ask why, don't you, Jake? Why the false Sicarius? We are such a visual society today, so quick to judge by appearances, so besotted by the superficialities of shape and form. You would agree with that, Dark,

would you not, my Beauty Salon Burner? One as physically nondescript as myself could never represent the
figure of Sicarius – not striking enough, insufficiently
photogenic for the world's vidnews bulletins – but I am
most assuredly the *mind* of Sicarius, and it is the mind
that matters.'

Yeah, right, Jake thought. So it was just as well the
twisted scumbag couldn't see into his.

But there was a problem. Two problems. Namely
Dravic and Orme. One of them was always by
Sicarius' side, always. Either Jake took a chance and
attacked the leader of the Bringers with one or other of
his bodyguards still in attendance, or he bided his time
until an opportunity arose that carried less risk of
failure.

As Sicarius seemed happy to remain at home base
for a few days, Jake opted for the latter. He wished he
could be sure his decision was purely the result of cold,
clinical mission calculations. And not the product of
fear that in the end he would prove too squeamish, too
soft to mete out to the terrorist what he so richly
deserved.

Sicarius was a sickness, Jake told himself. Jake Black
was the cure.

In the mean time he roamed the base and learned
more about his adversary. He had to admit that the
founder of the Bringers of the Night was a remarkable
man. Much of their equipment it seemed he had
designed himself. He could apparently speak a dozen
languages. He held doctorates in physics, chemistry, fine
arts and philosophy. He painted in oils, wrote sonnets

and made bombs. He was a scientist, a scholar, a genius, a true Renaissance man. Jake found himself pondering over the good Sicarius might have done had he dedicated himself to working for the benefit of humanity. Yet he was a merciless killer, devoted only to darkness and death.

'You are wondering what made me what I am,' the terrorist said one time. 'There comes a moment when all my followers wonder that, Jake, those with the intelligence to think for themselves.' He cast a pitying glance across to Orme who was standing nearby. 'They serve too, of course, who only follow orders.'

The three of them were in Sicarius' private quarters. These were spartanly furnished, as Jake might have anticipated, with the exception of the glossy grand piano that the terrorist leader was playing now. Jake was no aficionado of any music that didn't come with a drumbeat or a five-minute guitar solo, but the caressively tender manner with which Sicarius coaxed the keys to melody indicated even to him that many a concert pianist would have to bow to this man's skill.

'Perhaps you think a traumatic event in my past moulded me into my present form,' suggested Sicarius. 'Or indignation at some perceived injustice that took root in my soul and grew.'

'It's not my place to ask that kind of question, Sicarius,' said Jake humbly, though he wanted to know. He almost *needed* to know.

'Darkness raised me, Jake Denver. Once, when I was a child, I feared darkness. I believed that the night contained unspeakable terrors, monsters that lurked unseen in its black depths, that longed to seize me and torment me and drive me mad, and my only protection against them was the light. I could not sleep in my room without a light; I dared not. But my father scorned my fears. He told me there were no such things as monsters in the dark and he took my light away. He left me alone, defenceless, in darkness. And he was wrong because out of the blackness creatures came to me, and I covered my eyes but they tore my hands away and forced me to look at them, and I tried to cover my ears too but again they were too strong and I was compelled to listen to their words. But *I* was wrong also. Though I remember screaming at first, screaming until my throat cracked, in time I realised that the denizens of darkness were not monsters. They were my friends. They had things that they could teach me, sights that they could show me, and in time I no longer feared them. I *embraced* them, fully, fanatically, you might say. I gave them my hand willingly and they led me on. I became their son, I became Sicarius, and darkness leads me still.'

Jake began to realise why Sicarius wasn't out helping people somewhere. Crazy wasn't the word. Out of his head? Should be put out of his misery.

'I learned strange and wonderful things,' Sicarius said. I bet you did, you sick lunatic, thought Jake. 'For example, creation and destruction are the same. This piano, Denver. A beautiful object, is it not? A worthy tribute to its maker's creativity. And yet it was born with the death of a tree, one kind of beauty sacrificed for another, the exchange between creation and destruction not even noted. And the sounds that it makes, the music. Attend.' Sicarius played and there was suddenly gentleness and hope in the dark valley. Then he stopped. He stood. 'Your blaster, please, Orme.' Provided. 'And now, attend again.'

He fired at the piano. The instrument exploded, burst into crackling flames. Jake and even Orme flinched back. Sicarius did not.

'Other sounds, different music. And yet the same. Vibrations travelling through the air. No more, no less. This is what I have learned, that nothing has any greater value than anything else, and therefore the only thing of true worth is nothing*ness*. Oblivion. Blackness. Night. We are the Bringers of the Night,' concluded Sicarius, his face serene with his own conviction, 'and we say the age of false light is over. The time of darkness is near. Be glad, Jake Denver. The moment of our fulfilment is at hand.'

Jake was so engrossed in his own thoughts he didn't hear Dark's approach until she was sitting down beside him. Add lack of alertness to the list of cardinal sins he'd committed as an agent on active operations. His report card when he returned to Deveraux was hardly shaping up as top-of-the-class material. And correction: *if* he returned to Deveraux.

At least he felt on safe enough territory with Dark. 'Bit of a turn-up, isn't it?' Jake grinned. 'You choosing to eat with me rather than the other way round.' He'd hardly touched his food, in fact. The catering in the Bringers' dining area seemed a homage to that in Deepwater One.

Armies might well march on their stomach; seemed terrorists only needed their hate to keep them going.

'I can go somewhere else if you'd sooner,' bridled Dark with uncustomary petulance.

She wanted to talk. Jake read the signs. 'No. You're good.'

'I just thought, now that I've got the chance, I wanted to explain what happened back in the control centre.'

'How do you mean?' Jake would have preferred to forget what happened back at the control centre.

'My blaster jamming,' Dark expanded. 'It really did. I wanted to shoot those controllers, I wanted to be just like you and the others, to justify Null's – Sicarius' – faith in me, but . . . Only Orme's been looking at me oddly ever since, like he doesn't trust me or something, and some of the others too. Dravic.'

'So what do you want from me?'

'You don't think the same way as them, do you, Jake? You don't think badly of me?'

'Jake is it now? That's the first time you've called me by my first name. Must be serious.'

'Well if you're gonna be like that . . .' With an expression half hurt, half anger, Dark started to rise.

Jake's hand restrained her. Jake's hand on her hand. 'Okay. Okay. Don't go away mad. I'm sorry. Sit . . . that's better.' He gazed into her eyes. Seemed the shutters were opening, just a sliver, just a crack. He could almost glimpse another Dark beyond, a girl frightened and bewildered. 'So you didn't join in merrily mowing down a line of helpless techs at their consoles . . .'

'I wanted to. I did. But my blaster . . .'

'Why should that make me think badly of you? I don't.
I like you, Dark.'

'You do? Why?'

The question seemed genuine. It startled Jake. 'Why?
Uh . . . why not?'

'I'm not worth liking. I don't deserve it.' Dark was
bleak. 'If you really knew the kind of person I am, the
things I've done, you wouldn't like me. Nobody would.'

'Why not let me be the judge of that.' Jake felt something stirring inside him, something good. 'Tell me. You
can trust me. Promise. You could even tell me your real
name if you're feeling *really* daring, 'cause call me suspicious but I just don't reckon Dark puts in an appearance
on your birth certificate.'

'I don't know.' She looked at him cautiously, from
behind years of defences. 'I don't know if I can . . . I
don't understand you, Jake. You act like you belong
with the Bringers and yet there's something about you
that's different . . .'

Careful, Jake, he warned himself. Don't go too far.
Compromising his cover would be just about the perfect
end to a wonderful few days. Harden the expression.
Stern the voice. 'You're wrong, Dark. I'm the same.
Didn't you see me in the control centre while you were
fumbling with defective weaponry?'

'Yes, but . . .'

'Don't be mistaken, Dark. The night is in me, too.'

It seemed strange to think of Shakespeare when you
were lying in your bed in a room that was little more
than a cave with a door and part of a terrorist base

besides, particularly as Jake had never been what could be termed an active reader, certainly not of fancy plays in a kind of code English written by a guy in a frilly collar five hundred years ago. But he'd always kind of liked *Macbeth*. It was the blood, he supposed, the murders, the out, brief candles. He remembered reading it through with Lori one summer afternoon, him as Macbeth and her as everyone else, and they'd been sprawled on the grass in the grounds of Spy High and the sun had been squintingly bright above them and there'd been laughter and plenty of interruptions while lips were put to uses other than phrasing poetry, and the moral dilemma of the would-be king of Scotland had seemed to him mere words upon a page.

Didn't seem that way now.

Macbeth murdered the rightful ruler of his country to become king himself. Now while Jake's mission was about assassination, there was no parallel between Macbeth's victim and Sicarius. King Duncan was a good man – Shakespeare had gone to great pains to point that out – while the leader of the Bringers was a ruthless terrorist whose demise would no doubt lead to global celebrations. The play didn't bother Jake from that point of view. What troubled him here in the dark was the effect of his actions on Macbeth himself. Before he killed in cold blood he was a man capable of both good and evil, it seemed. Afterwards, evil slowly, inevitably consumed him. The murder of the king changed him, for ever. There was no undoing it once it was done, no going back. It was as if he had become a different man.

Jake thought fearfully: what if the same thing should happen to him?

What if it didn't matter that the assassination of Sicarius was arguably justifiable? What did 'arguably' *mean*? That somebody wasn't sure. It was like their old Ethics in Espionage classes: would it be right, if you could travel through time, to go back to Hitler's childhood and kill him, thereby preventing the rise of the Nazis, the Holocaust, etc? Would it be right? *Arguably*. Maybe yes, maybe no. It seemed to Jake that the effect on *him* of what he'd been ordered to do could be the same whether or not anyone else agreed or disagreed with the course of action. *Now* he was a secret agent with a temper and a sense of injustice. *Then* he'd be an assassin with a body count.

Which did he want to be? Would he lose Jake Daly somewhere along the way? Had he *already* lost him?

Because what choice did he truly have? He was a Deveraux operative in the field. He had his orders. It was his responsibility to carry them out, and he never shirked his responsibilities.

Jake Black got up. He retrieved his shock blaster from where he'd left it. The weapon was not switched to Stun. He did not turn on the light. He'd memorised the route from his own room to those of Sicarius already so that he could make his way there in the dark.

So that no one could see what he was going to do.

Jake moved through tunnels with profound silence, in a deaf world. He felt he was deep underground and the surface and the sky an unscalable distance above him. He moved like oil.

Now was the time. While Sicarius was sleeping. While he was helpless in his bed

(The culmination of his training, of four years of work at Deveraux, to shoot a man sleeping in his bed. Would his parents be proud if they knew? Sicarius' victims, if *they* knew: would they be glad?)

Jake was one with the darkness, approaching the door.

He would creep to the bedside, soundless. He could come upon Sicarius like a dream. He would aim his blaster, press it perhaps against the man's forehead, as his hand now pressed against the cool wood of the door.

His finger would tighten on the trigger. It only took the action of a muscle to end a life.

But what if Sicarius woke? What if his eyes opened and they would be staring and white if they did that and could Jake look him in the eye and still squeeze the trigger?

He paused at the door. He paused on the threshold.

Someone was coming. From inside.

Jake withdrew into the sheltering blackness. In time to prevent both himself and Dravic from getting an unpleasant surprise. The angular man closed the door softly enough behind him but made no attempt to move elsewhere. A collar with a name-tag hung around his neck couldn't have made it more obvious. Guard-dog. Sicarius' loyal lieutenant evidently kept watch 24/7.

Jake could take Dravic out but then Sicarius might hear the shot. If he heard the shot he could raise the alarm. If he raised the alarm Jake's mission might still be foiled.

It was the logic of inaction, the reasoning of retreat. Jake backed away, as silently as ever and not at all with relief. The option of removing Dravic as an obstacle with his bare hands and therefore not risking alerting Sicarius at all he was certain later had never occurred to him. There'd be other opportunities, clearer chances.

Besides, he was intrigued by what the terrorist had declared before, that the moment of their fulfilment was at hand. What did that mean? What exactly was Sicarius planning?

He had a feeling Jonathan Deveraux would want to know.

Somebody was in his room. By now Jake's eyes had adapted to the lack of light. He could see the intruder, his outline a bolder black against the prevailing darkness. Instinct took over. Jake was diving to the floor, forward-rolling, springing up, smashing into the figure, pinning his arms as they fell across the bed.

She squealed.

Not *his* outline. Not *his* arms. *Hers*.

Dark's.

Flipping on the light proved it.

'Jake, what did you do *that* for?'

'What do you think? How was I to know who was in my room in the middle of the night? You could have been, I don't know, a spy or something, an agent sent by the authorities to infiltrate us.'

'Oh, sure. That's likely.' After their brief tussle, Dark's hair looked even more unkempt than usual. 'Where've you been, anyway? Like you say, it *is* the middle of the night. And with your shock blaster.'

'I was just checking security.' If assassination was as easy as lying, Sicarius would be history by now. 'You can never be too careful.' And quickly change the subject. 'But what are you doing here, Dark?'

'I was lonely,' she confessed. 'I needed some company. Thought you might too.'

'I'm not really up to a conversation or a game of cards right now, Dark.' He needed to think.

'It wasn't that kind of company I had in mind.' And she was suddenly pressing against him, awkwardly, like she'd tripped and stumbled. Her mouth was very close to his.

'Ah, what's going on?'

'You said you liked me.'

'I did. I mean, yeah, I said that. I do like you.'

'So now you can prove it.'

'No. No. I don't think so. Dark . . .' Jake held up his hands, tried to put space between them without seeming harsh. It wasn't easy. 'This isn't a good idea.'

'Isn't it what you want?' She sounded hurt. 'You said you liked me.'

'That wasn't the cue for an immediate head and shoulders.'

'I thought that was what all boys wanted . . .'

'Maybe you need to start hanging with a better class of boy. We're not all sleazes after just one thing.'

'Are you not?' Dark's eyes flashed with old rage. She jerked herself away from Jake. 'I know what it is. It's the way I look, isn't it? Not exactly Beauty Queen of the

Month, huh, Jake? Not quite Miss USA 2066. Miss Teen Ugly, maybe, but—'

'Whoa. Whoa. You're putting yourself down. Don't put yourself down.' And inside him, seeing her perched desolately on the bed, there was an instinct to hug Dark, to comfort her. But he was afraid such an action might be misinterpreted. 'I'm not talking about appearances, I'm not interested in what you think you look like. I'm talking about inside. I'm talking about you, Dark, about who you are and who you want to be, the kind of person you want to be.'

'What you see is what you get,' Dark mocked. 'Which obviously isn't much.'

'That's exactly what I mean. You mustn't talk like that. Value yourself. Respect yourself. Us being together now isn't right not because I don't like you but because I *do*.'

'Is that supposed to make sense, Jake?'

'You're worth more than a quick fumble, Dark, a lot more. Everybody is. It's obvious you've had bad times before, but if you want to talk . . .'

'I'm sorry.' Dark jumped to her feet. 'Conversations are out and I'm sure you must be tired after all that pontificating, Jake. Sorry to have disturbed you. I'll go.'

She went. As far as the door.

'Dark . . .' But he couldn't quite bring himself to call her back.

Espionage work, they'd always been taught, was like a maze. Sometimes an agent's progress through it might be blocked by a dead end. Sometimes there might appear to be so many dead ends in their path that the way forward seemed hopeless, their mission doomed to failure. But they'd been taught never to give up. Every maze had a way through. It was only a matter of finding it.

So the Jake Black file was now officially useless in helping Lori and Bex trace its subject. Jake was no longer imprisoned in Deepwater One. His bio-signature and the Deveraux surveillance satellites were unlikely to be helpful this time either. Jake could be anywhere in the world, and not even the Spy High budget was sky high enough to cover that kind of ground, *even* if they could initiate a search without Mr Deveraux's knowledge.

Dead ends. Try another way.

The two girls sat at the computer in a Boston apartment apparently rented by a Ms Rebecca Dee, who had pleasantly surprised the landlord by paying cash. Even for the heir to the Deveraux fortune, it hadn't been easy to come up with the six months' advance rent in such an old-fashioned form, but the usual credit transfer would have been too easy to trace.

They'd hacked into the prison authorities' records and were scrutinising every scrap of information available regarding the Bringer of the Night named Null.

It wasn't going well.

'If I read another psychiatrist's report on Null concluding childhood trauma and recommending intensive counselling to help him come to terms with it and, quote, facilitate his readmission into the wider community, unquote,' grumbled Bex, 'I'll be the one catching a transfer sub to a Deepwater. For wiping out the entire psychiatric community of the East Coast. I think there are three little words I'd like to whisper in your shell-like, Lo: I give up.'

'We can't give up,' Lori said disapprovingly, even though she knew her friend was expressing general dismay rather than serious intent. 'We *know* Jake made contact with Null. There's got to be something here that'll give us a clue as to where they might be.'

Bex pressed a key. 'Hey, here's Null's reading list. Maybe if there are travel books we can at least narrow it down to a country.'

'Bex, you're a genius.'

'Lori, I was joking.'

'Me too. But listen' – Lori's blue eyes sparkled – 'you know Eddie's into twentieth-century cinema, one of his big favourite movies is – oh, it's a number. Five. Six.'

'Seven?'

'I was getting there. Cop movie. Serial killer. They track him down by checking library data to see who'd borrowed certain types of books, books that somebody committing the kind of murders the detectives were trying to solve might well have read. In this case, religious stuff—'

'Lo, we haven't got time for a review. The point?'

'Null's books. The ones he was reading in prison. *They're* the something. Look at those titles. Quantum physics. Dimensional engineering.'

'Bit of a boff on the quiet, our Null,' said Bex. 'Must be hard to find the time to read, you know, in between blowing people up and stuff.'

'And a fan of this Professor L.A. Seerborn.' Lori took

over at the keyboard, did some quick cross-referencing. 'In fact, Null's read everything Professor Landon Seerborn has ever published.'

'So?'

'He's a physicist. Doesn't seem to do much now. A little bit of teaching at the University of Pennsylvania.'

'And at the risk of getting boring, so?'

'So there's a connection. Null and Seerborn. I can feel it. I know it.' Lori grinned at her friend. 'What are we waiting for? Professor Seerborn's next class just expanded by two.'

'You have been patient, my disciples of darkness,' said Sicarius, 'but now your patience will be rewarded. The time of waiting is over.'

The Bringers had been gathered together by their leader like some kind of oversubscribed Last Supper. Jake noted that Dark was on the opposite side of the room to him, not by accident, and that she was fiercely refusing to look at him. He didn't like to think that by rejecting her advances last night he'd somehow confirmed her cynical view of human – and especially male – nature, but right now he reckoned he had more to think about than Dark. Outside, the helicopters were landing. Inside, the terrorists' cache of arms awaited distribution.

Whatever Sicarius had in mind, the planning stage seemed just about over.

'We embark on an enterprise unlike any other in the history of our kind.' And he sure knew how to build it up. 'We are the Bringers of the Night and the time has come to truly *earn* our name. Night will fall upon the earth and it will be total and it will be absolute and it will be eternal. We will *make* it so. It is our destiny.'

Destiny nothing. Jake wanted to know details.

'First, however,' Sicarius added, 'we must pay a visit to an old friend . . .'

NINE

From the University of Pennsylvania Prospectus, 2066 edition

Situated among rolling hills and verdant woodland, the University of Pennsylvania is the perfect place to study. Its facilities across the full range of academic disciplines are, as would be expected, state of the art, but it is the ambience of the university's surroundings that its freshmen first tend to comment on, their peacefulness, their tranquillity, the sense that an idyllic, harmonious haven has been established here eminently conducive to learning and far away from the noise and distractions of the modern world.

They burst into the lecture theatre with pulse rifles blazing. Sicarius and Dravic didn't need to be shouting 'Out! Out!' at the tops of their voices. The students slumped in the long rows of seating probably required little encouragement to leave for the cafeteria or bar at the best of times, and to be roused from a stupor while old Seerborn droned on about protons and antiprotons by fanatics brandishing automatic weapons certainly failed to qualify as one of those.

There were screams. There was panic. There was a wild, frantic scramble for the doors.

'See how they care only for themselves,' observed Dravic to Jake conversationally. 'See how they tear at those ahead of them, clamber and climb over their backs, trample the fallen in their desperation to escape. Yet less than a minute ago they would have claimed that the boy or the girl whose head they now tread into the floor was a friend.'

Something you'll never catch me saying about *you*, scumbag, thought Jake grimly. But at least there were not going to be fatalities here. Sicarius had ordered the gunfire as a scare tactic, simply to clear the theatre. It wasn't the students that concerned him. It was their teacher.

Professor Landon Seerborn blinked myopically as the armed intruders advanced upon him. He hadn't dared join the crush at the doors. He was old, frail, he tended to shake even when not faced with the business ends of a dozen pulse rifles. If whoever these people were wanted him dead, there wasn't much he could do about it.

'Relax, Professor Seerborn,' Sicarius said soothingly as he, Dravic and Jake closed in. Dark had gone to guard the doors with the rest of the group. 'We don't intend to shoot you. Not unless you give us no choice.'

'Who are you?' the old man croaked. 'How do you know my name?'

'We can't talk here,' said Sicarius. 'I imagine it's much cosier in your study.'

'You won't get away with this. Campus security —'

'Will have problems of their own, Professor.'

It was impossible to describe the student *type* these days, the librarian reflected. At one time you could pick them out a mile away, fresh-faced girls with plaits and big scarves, diffident boys with spectacles, bad hair and worse chat-up lines; at the other end of the scale, lantern-jawed blond hulks who could scarcely write their names but were a shoo-in for the university football team. The Universal Education Act had changed all that. Now you could study (broadly speaking) at the finest educational establishments in the country without any qualifications at all. The British had led the way in the early part of the century. The librarian had to admit that she did not approve. Standards, she thought, standards.

Take this gentleman standing before her now, or rather *slouching* before her. She had to admit that she'd always disapproved of shaven heads, but even so, the fellow still appeared highly inappropriate material for the University of Pennsylvania. His companions, too, most of them looking like they'd been released from jail that very morning.

'Can I help you, sir?' she said, with a professional courtesy she did not feel.

'Not me,' said Shaven-Head, 'but you can help yourself.'

'I'm sorry? I don't quite —'

'Leave. The library. Leave the library.'

'I don't . . .' The librarian considered pressing her panic button. She didn't approve of this brute at all. And what was that, drifting to her from outside? The sound of screaming? 'Who are you?'

'Well, you know like builders, people who put things up.' Orme grinned. 'We're more like the opposite.'

It was hushed a little by distance, but gunfire and explosions still reached the ears of those in Seerborn's study.

'It seems Orme's diversion is well under way,' commented Sicarius. 'Something of a tribute to your earlier exploits, hmm, Denver? Let the library become the funeral pyre for the light of learning.'

'You're mad,' uttered Professor Landon Seerborn. 'You're *evil*.'

They'd bound the old man to his chair. 'So you don't tire yourself out moving about,' Dravic had explained. 'See? We've only got your welfare at heart.'

Now Sicarius crouched down by the Professor's side. 'Good and evil, sanity and insanity, relative concepts as you well know, Professor. Was the man who invented the wheel evil because so many lives have been crushed beneath carts and cars over the years? Was Einstein evil because his genius helped create the atomic bomb? Are *you* evil, Professor Seerborn, for pioneering the science of dimensional engineering?' Sicarius smiled slyly. 'Am *I* evil, for seeking to advance it further?'

Seerborn frowned. 'What can a man like you know of dimensional engineering?'

Jake was wondering the same. The books in Sicarius' cell. More vitally, though, he was trying to figure out the link between dimensional engineering, if that was what had brought the terrorists here, and the total, absolute, eternal night that Sicarius had promised. Some kind of big bomb, maybe, more destructive than the atom bomb? He wished his leader was a little more forthcoming with his followers as to the exact nature of his plans.

Sicarius was chuckling like somebody who'd just noticed the obituary of an old enemy. 'Don't you remember me, Professor? I was in your quantum physics class, oh, it must be twenty years ago now.'

'Impossible!' scoffed the old man.

'No, I distinctly recall you praising me on more than one occasion for possessing – I recollect the words precisely – "one of the most fearless and original minds it has been my pleasure to encounter for many a year". You said I used to ask the questions that no one else would dare.'

'Nonsense,' denied Seerborn. 'This is sheer nonsense.'

But Jake guessed it was true.

'I have a question for you now, Professor,' said Sicarius, 'and I have come a long way for the answer. Where is IDEA?'

Lori and Bex had downloaded maps and floor-plans of the University of Pennsylvania into the navigation computers of their SkyBikes. Specify the required destination, Professor Landon Seerborn's private study, and their machines would fly them there automatically.

All the girls needed to do was hold on to the handlebars and enjoy the ride.

The first inkling they had that matters might not proceed so smoothly was the police wheellesses streaking past them in the same direction, lights flashing and sirens wailing.

'Do you get the feeling we might be a little too late?' said Lori.

'Maybe it's just a party got out of hand,' Bex suggested.

'At eleven thirty in the morning?'

'Lo, these are students we're talking about here.'

The security cordon that was springing up around the perimeter of the campus indicated a situation more serious than a few overexuberant revellers. A couple of cops tried to wave the Deveraux agents down. Instead, Lori and Bex lifted their bikes higher. No time for explanations. No time for delays.

'This isn't a coincidence,' Lori scowled, 'us arriving just in time for a major security alert.' Below them, students, faculty members, administrative staff, the entire university population, it seemed, were in hectic flight from the campus. 'Somehow, this is about Seerborn. We've got to find him.'

The certainty was like steel in her mind. Find Landon Seerborn and you find Jake.

'Lori!' Bex cried, appalled. 'The library!'

One of the most prestigious buildings in the university, according to the prospectus. Ten storeys high, housing a collection of over a million volumes in book form alone, ignoring the vast resources stored on disk and the holo-transfer facilities to access libraries elsewhere in the world. Fronted by a gleaming glass façade that was kept so polished it hardly seemed to be there at all. Which was the point. The knowledge and wisdom and wit of Mankind were openly available to everyone. Including, it seemed, as Lori too now stared aghast, those who scarcely appreciated it.

The library was in flames.

There were still people inside, people at the mercy of killers with guns.

Find Landon Seerborn, the notion refused to vacate Lori's brain, and you find Jake.

'Lori, where?'

Seerborn's study was the other side of campus.

'Where do you think, Bex?' Lori switched her bike to manual, steered it towards the library. 'We've got lives to save.'

Seerborn would have to wait.

'Sorry, Professor.' Sicarius leaned closer to the old man's trembling lips. 'I'm afraid I can't hear you.'

'I said I have no idea what you're talking about.'

'Is that supposed to be a pun? If it is, it's in poor taste.' Sicarius' eyes narrowed threateningly. 'You know as well as I do that IDEA is an acronym. The International Dimensional Engineering Agency. You know because you were not only the organisation's co-founder but also a major contributor to its early breakthroughs.'

Seerborn opted to exchange feigned ignorance for stubborn defensiveness. 'What if I was?'

'Ah, Professor, there's no need to be bashful. The advances that have been made in the field of dimensional engineering thanks to your genius! The science to construct a bridge between not worlds, but universes!' Sicarius warmed to his theme. 'Astonishing. A discovery of boundless potential. Also, of course, of considerable danger. I assume the fear of unfortunate mishaps occurring during the course of your work was behind your original decision to site IDEA's research facility well away from areas of significant population, Professor, yes? Though I would have thought, personally, that the ignorant masses would have clamoured for the privilege to perish in the name of human progress, wouldn't you? But then I suppose that lack of imagination is what makes them ignorant masses in the first place.'

'You're deranged,' observed Professor Landon Seerborn.

'There are only *so* many ways you can impugn my sanity,' said Sicarius.

'Leader!' Dravic alerted the terrorist to a subtle change in the note of violence issuing from the library. It sounded now as if battle had been joined.

Whoever was taking Orme on, Jake thought, needed to eliminate him fast. If they did, there was a chance Sicarius could be stopped right here, right now.

The possibility did not pass the Bringers' founder by. 'It appears our time together may be briefer than I would have liked, Professor. So. Two years ago IDEA was moved elsewhere, to a secret location. This implies to me that even then its work was close to fruition, your dream of spanning the dimensions on the brink of fulfilment. The promise of reward at its greatest; so too the prospect of disaster. I have recently been engaged in the development of dimensional engineering theories of my own, Professor, humble extensions to your researches, naturally, but now I feel I am in a position to move from theory into practice. To do that, however, I need access to IDEA. Where is it, Professor? Where is the facility now?'

'I don't know,' Seerborn said stubbornly. 'And if I *did* know —'

'You wouldn't tell me.' Sicarius sighed wearily. 'But you *do*, Seerborn, and you *will*.'

'You can't force me,' the Professor said defiantly.

'Oh, I think we can.' Sicarius produced a thin metal object that resembled a cattle prod. He activated it and the tip glowed a fiery red. Everyone in the study could feel its heat.

Seerborn's eyes widened. He struggled uselessly against his bonds. 'Even *you* wouldn't torture an old man . . .'

'Of course not,' said Sicarius. He passed the device to his loyal lieutenant. 'Dravic, on the other hand . . .'

Lori and Bex swooped towards the glass front of the library. Beyond it, the carnage of combusting books as several terrorist types wielding flame-throwers turned shelves into bonfires. They must have disabled the sprinkler system, Lori thought. Other aggressors seemed satisfied with more conventional arms, pulse and shock blasts pocking ceilings and floors. The girls could see students and staff scrambling hectically for cover, some still clutching books to their chests like the volumes were lives to be saved. At the moment the attackers appeared more interested in sheer wanton destruction rather than racking up a body count, but that could change at any moment – unless the Deveraux agents did something about it.

'We going in?' Bex called across needlessly.

Lori nodded. 'I'll take up. You take down.'

'Aren't we going through the door?'

'No time. We'll make our own door.'

'The local glazier's gonna think Christmas has come early,' grinned Bex. She brought her SkyBike's missile systems on-line. 'Fifth floor looks clear.'

They fired in perfect union. The glass façade shattered with a sound as if every bottle in the world had been smashed simultaneously. It tore at the ears of those inside the library as excruciatingly as claws raking a blackboard, but Lori and Bex were not distracted. They would require all their concentration now to keep their SkyBikes from colliding with shelves, floors and ceilings. The machines weren't really intended for indoor use.

They streaked into the building regardless.

First target. Female terrorist directly ahead of Lori. Shock blasters in both hands. Slow to react with either. Sleepshot sent her spinning backwards. Just as well for *her* sake. Two seconds later and if she'd still been standing Lori's bike would have taken her head off.

A comrade who looked more simian than human rushing up the stairs. Sighted Bex while she was at the far end of a narrow aisle between rows of surprisingly undamaged books. Undamaged so far. The simian's quickly deployed pulse rifle was certain to change that. But while she disapproved of damaging property, Bex liked the idea of injuring people even less, particularly when the individual in question was herself.

Second time in less than a week that she'd faced a crucial confrontation in a library. Whoever said they were boring places?

Little room to manoeuvre side to side as Bex boosted her bike towards the Bad Guy. Shelves were like the walls of an alley. There was more flexibility up and down. She needed it. Pulse blasts scorching below her, then searing just above her head. Her machine was sensitive to the slightest pressure on its handlebars. She held it steady with her left hand, releasing her right to take aim. Her sleepshot wristband flashed.

Simian descended the stairs even more rapidly than he'd climbed them.

Bex followed, taking out two more terrorists who'd gathered rather foolishly at the bottom of the stairwell. She hoped Lori was doing as well.

Two floors up, the history section, and the whoosh of the flame-thrower reminded Lori of her adventure on St Dominguez a while back, putting an end to the Judson family's plan to assassinate President Westwood. Why were there people like that in the world? People who created ugliness instead of beauty? People who loved death instead of life?

People like the shaven-headed man ahead of her, igniting books recording the events of hundreds of years with the fanatical zeal of one who would as soon torch the years themselves and plunge Man back into the Dark Ages.

Maybe it was balance, Lori thought. Without the existence of evil, how could you recognise good? Without darkness, how would you know light?

Probably best to pause with the philosophical considerations for the time being. At least until she'd tipped this particular balance in her favour. Shaven-Head had seen her though he didn't recognise her. Lori knew him. His picture was in the Deepwater files. Orme. One of Null's followers.

Jake had to be nearby too. Her heart raced.

Her reflexes were pretty quick also. Needed to be. The spout of fire from Orme's weapon was stingingly close. The Ming Dynasties to her left were suddenly ablaze. She couldn't tackle him head on, the flame-thrower's killing arc was too wide. She gunned her bike towards the Italian Renaissance, possibly in the hope that a little of that period's creative ingenuity might rub off on her and provide a means of defeating Orme.

Who seemed almost impervious to fire. He pursued her manically through the burning aisles, yelling words she couldn't hear but which were unlikely to be complimentary. Jets of flame made her flight an inferno. The lives of Michelangelo and Leonardo de Vinci, incinerated in a moment. Dante. The Medicis. Cremated.

Lori hoped the Industrial Revolution might give her some shelter. It was all right for her vehicle: SkyBikes didn't blister, couldn't be overcome by smoke. And then, of course, she realised what to do.

She veered around sharply. Orme was on his way. Red fire at the barrel of the flame-thrower like it was licking its lips in anticipation. Lori pointed her SkyBike directly at him, accelerated.

As she felt the speed increasing, she threw herself off.

Orme raised the flame-thrower, realised it would do no good. He instinctively back-pedalled. No good either, not with the riderless bike almost upon him. Third option: leap out of its path. If he'd done that first, he might have been all right. As it was, he crashed into already teetering shelving which seized its opportunity to wreak some small revenge on the book-burner by completing its collapse on top of him.

Dazed, Orme saw the blonde girl sprinting towards him. She was fast, but if he could just reach his flame-thrower she'd still be toast.

Lori's booted foot prevented him. 'Be grateful you still have the use of your other five fingers,' she said, 'and hey, did no one ever tell you it's dangerous to play with fire?'

'Who are you?' Orme demanded.

'Who I am doesn't matter.' Lori straddled the man's chest, keeping him helpless. 'Who *you* are, on the other hand . . . Where's Null?'

Orme chuckled as if at some secret joke. The laugh quickly became a cough. The smoke was thickening as the fire took hold. 'You gotta get me out of here. Get me out of here or we'll fry.'

'Not so brave without a nice big flame-thrower in your hands, huh, Orme?' The heat was becoming intense now but Lori resisted it. 'Out of here, second. Null, first. Where? Here in the library with you?'

'With Seerborn. With Professor Landon Seerborn.'

Sicarius led the way to the roof. Jake and Dark were close behind him, the rest of the Bringers following with Dravic in the rear. They moved with urgency.

'It was almost a pleasure seeing him again,' the terrorist leader still managed to reflect. 'I do hope they do him justice in the obituary columns.'

Jake gritted his teeth as he climbed the stairs. He should have done something, even though to have attempted to save Seerborn would have certainly terminated his mission and probably his life into the bargain. His head told him that he'd been wise not to protest or make a stand. The greater good, his head told him, was best served by the sacrifice of one man here if it meant saving dozens, maybe hundreds later on. But his heart wasn't having it. His heart refused to accept that life and death could be subject to cold calculation. His heart was seething with rage and shame.

He should have *done* something.

The old man had looked at him, and his weak, rheumy eyes had failed to distinguish between Jake and the heartless killers amongst whom he was hiding. Seerborn had noticed no difference. Perhaps there no longer was one.

How he was feeling now, it would be another part of the payback when Jake finally faced Sicarius alone.

They spilled out on to the roof. The helicopter Dravic had signalled was already hovering high above them. As

they emerged, its undercarriage opened and the telltale
blue light of a tractor beam flashed downwards.

'Quickly,' instructed Sicarius. 'Time is obviously now
of the essence. We must be about our business.'

'We're not leaving the others?' Dark apparently har-
boured some misguided notion of group loyalty.

'They have served their purpose,' Sicarius declared,
entering the tractor beam. 'They are no longer necessary.' He ascended to the helicopter like one of the elect
into Heaven.

'Yes would have done,' muttered Jake, but he'd be
glad to leave the university himself. What he'd allowed to
happen here had done him no credit.

Jake stepped into the tractor beam.

'They're getting away!' Bex cried. 'Faster, you geriatric
hunk of tin. Faster!'

But SkyBikes were not designed to give chase to helicopters. By the time she'd gained the Faculty of Science
building, the helicopter containing maybe Null, maybe
Jake, maybe Seerborn – because it *had* to belong to the
Bringers of the Night – was already soaring out of
range. Anyway, even if *she* could have maintained any
kind of pursuit, Lori would have been left behind. Her
bike was still functional, but its left rear propulsion unit
had been damaged by Orme's flame-thrower.

Bex swore. Unladylike, yes, but therapeutic.
Sometimes four letters were all you needed.

She landed on the rooftop where she'd seen the tractor
beam at work. The door to the stairwell was open.
Professor Seerborn's study was two floors down. That

was where Orme had told Lori his comrades were taking the old man. Some comrades, she thought, out of here without a second thought for the group in the library – not that they were in any condition to go anywhere right now, she and Lori had seen to that. She signed to her partner that she was going in. Could be Null had left a clue or something.

'No! Bex! Wait!' Lori could have saved her breath. Possibly the piercings in her ears had had a detrimental effect on the blue-haired girl's hearing, or even on her memory. Had she forgotten that team-mates were supposed to *work* as a team? Bex might be rushing into a trap.

Lori was off her bike almost before it had set down. She took the stairs three at a time. Two floors down. Left from the stairwell. Third on the right The floor-plans matched the reality precisely. A study. Professor L.A. Seerborn. But diagrams had not prepared her for what awaited inside.

The professor, bound and gagged in his chair but apparently unharmed, straining against the ropes, sweat streaming down his forehead. Bex, ashen-faced, staring, but not at Seerborn.

At the bomb that was sitting patiently on the man's desk. The time-bomb that was ticking its time away.

The bomb that was less than a minute from detonation.

TEN

'**W**hat are you waiting for, Bex?' Lori yelled. 'Get rid of it!' Immobility was never much of a defence against a bomb.

'*No.*' Bex's voice carried the authority of her father. 'There's enough gelignite concentrate in that thing to blow half the campus.'

'Defuse?'

'Not in fifty seconds.'

Lori drew her belt-blade from its pouch in her mission belt. 'Get your SkyBike down here.' Her turn to take the lead. '*Now.*'

Bex did as she was told, pressed the stud on her belt that sent out a homing signal and activated her bike's automatic drive systems. Lori was cutting at Professor Seerborn's bonds. 'Don't worry, Professor. Everything's gonna be just fine.'

For the next forty seconds.

'I'd duck behind the desk if I were you,' Bex advised. Her SkyBike smashed through the window. Shards of glass and jagged splinters of wood spewed across the study. The girls were safely shielded by Seerborn's desk, however, and Lori had dragged the old man to the floor with her.

He pulled the gag from his mouth. 'The bomb. The *bomb*!'

'Not too articulate for a prof, is he?' Bex commented. 'Though he has a point. Lo?'

Was on her feet. The bomb in one hand. A length of the rope that had tied Seerborn in the other. To the saddle of the bike she lashed the former with the latter. Didn't have time for fancy knots.

Twenty seconds.

'Of *course*.' Bex was beside her, swiftly setting an automatic flight pattern. One way. Straight up. 'You think it'll get high enough before the big bang?'

'We'll find out in fifteen,' noted Lori grimly. She stepped back from the bike.

'And awaay we go.' Bex only hoped the bomb was secure.

The SkyBike threaded its way through the ruined window. As soon as it was clear of the building it streaked into the blue, accelerating, climbing, distancing. Lori and Bex thrust their heads through the gaping hole to observe its progress. It was a miniature, a speck, a mote. It could no longer be seen.

Detonation.

The bright flare of the explosion blinded them, its sound buffeting them like the gust of a hurricane. It sent the girls staggering back into the study. But their plan had worked. The bomb might well have been full of sound and fury, Lori thought, for some reason remembering summer afternoons reading *Macbeth* with Jake, but thanks to her and Bex it still signified nothing.

She crouched by the ailing Professor Seerborn, helped him up. It wasn't yet the time for self-congratulation. 'It's okay, Professor. You can relax now.' She guided him to his chair.

'Lo.' Bex had returned to the window. 'We've got cops on the way. Make it quick or we'll have some explaining to do.'

'Who are you girls?' Seerborn seemed disorientated. 'I don't understand any of this.'

'We're special services,' Lori lied. 'Professor, we need to know what happened.'

'Terrorists. Madmen. One of them said he was my student.'

'Was one of them young, my age, black hair, kind of intense?'

'Yes. Yes. He was one of them.'

Lori glanced relievedly at Bex. Jake. Alive. Undercover. They were still in the game.

'They threatened to torture me. If I didn't tell them.' Seerborn's voice was growing weaker by the second. 'Why won't my hands stop shaking? So I told them. I was afraid. I was a coward.'

'No, Professor.' Lori comforted the old man.

'He's going into shock, Lo.' Bex joined her.

The blonde girl nodded. 'What did you tell them, Professor?' she coaxed.

'I shouldn't have done it. I should have died before I did it but I was afraid.' Quivering fingers clutched at

Lori's arm. 'I told them where to find IDEA. I was a coward. I've placed the power of IDEA in the hands of a madman.'

'Idea?' Bex frowned. 'What's he talking about?'

Lori ignored her partner for once. 'Professor,' she said, 'what power?'

The old man's lips trembled. 'The power to destroy us all.'

A hot, dry wind swept across the plain. Most of the Bringers of the Night remained alongside the assault helicopter, like children not wishing to be parted from their mother. Most children, however, did not pass their time checking munitions while dressed in black stealth outfits. Sicarius, Dravic and Jake wore the same, but dared to wander. The sand swirled around them by the wind did not appear to bother Sicarius. Jake wouldn't allow it to trouble him either. From above they must have looked like beetles or dark stains on the land.

'Dravic, my most loyal lieutenant. Denver, my newest and most promising acolyte.' Sicarius wasn't usually big on compliments, Jake thought. What was going on? 'You are both more intelligent than the others. You will be able more fully to appreciate the scope of what I have planned. It is time to talk to you about IDEA.'

The terrorist hesitated then, became absorbed by a rocky ochre landscape that Jake would have categorised as hostile. The desert regions of Asia Minor had never done much for him. Sicarius, however, seemed elevated by his surroundings, as if in the parched, desolate emptiness he saw something of his own purpose. 'Perhaps Alexander the Great passed this way on his march to Persepolis,' he hypothesised at last, 'over two thousand years ago. Alexander, the greatest conqueror of them all. And now we are here, following in his footsteps, yet the Bringers of the Night have within our grasp the means to change the world more fundamentally and more profoundly than any warrior, king or conqueror before us. *Dimensional engineering.*'

The way he spoke the words, with a kind of lurid longing, chilled Jake despite the day's heat.

'It is said that when Alexander and his armies reached the limits of the known world the great king cried because there were no more lands to conquer. It seems Alexander knew much about warfare but little about geography and less about science. For now we know that the physical realm consists not simply of a single universe but of many, a multiverse, and we know that other dimensions exist in parallel with our own. New dimensions, strange dimensions, for so long beyond our reach. Until now. Until the science of dimensional engineering.'

'You mean,' frowned Jake, 'they've discovered a way for us to enter another dimension?'

'Look upon it more,' said Sicarius, 'as a way for another dimension to enter ours. The theory is this. Every chemical element is composed of atoms, and at the nucleus, at the heart of every atom, is the proton, the tiniest of all particles, without which no matter could exist. Protons are the key to all creation. Now our own universe was formed by an indescribably massive release of energy known by scientists as the Big Bang. If that kind of energy can be replicated – and *controlled* – we might be able to tear a hole in the very fabric of our universe and open a portal, a bridge, if you prefer, to another dimension.'

'Big Bang 2: A New Dimension,' Jake joked feebly.

Dravic offered no vocal reaction. He was listening to his leader as raptly as a devout church-goer to a particularly uplifting sermon.

'The effect could be achieved,' Sicarius continued, 'through the use of a particle accelerator. Think of *that* as a kind of racetrack around which would whirl countless numbers of protons, tens of thousands of times a second. Into this environment would then be inserted an equal measure of *anti*protons, the antimatter opposites of protons. Into the *same* particle accelerator, racing around the same track at the same speed, but in the *opposite* direction. If this was done, Denver, what do you think would be the result?'

'I guess a lot of little bangs,' Jake conjectured. 'And I guess lots of little bangs make one —'

'Exactly,' confirmed Sicarius. 'Collisions. Between protons and antiprotons, millions of collisions a second, disrupting matter at a sub-atomic level, unleashing the titanic energies that first created this universe from chaos. And as a direct consequence, the opening to other dimensions would be engineered. Dimensional engineering.'

'If you were planning on building a particle accelerator thing to do all that, though,' Jake said, 'it'd have to be kind of big, wouldn't it?'

'Oh, I can assure you it is, Denver,' Sicarius said with relish. 'How "kind of big" you will shortly discover, for thanks to the late Professor Seerborn's directions, we will soon be in possession of just such an accelerator. The scientists at IDEA have already built one. I suspect they have already created the interface between dimensions. My own calculations suggest that to have done so is more than possible. And I have made other calculations too.' The terrorist turned from Jake and Dravic. He stood against the wind on the lonely plain like a Biblical prophet. 'From order to chaos. From light to darkness. Absolute night is upon us now.'

Jake wasn't sure if it was his imagination, but it seemed to him that Dark was allowing her glance to stray in his direction again, for the first time since their unfortunate misunderstanding in his room. He hoped so. Maybe he'd been masquerading as a Bringer of the Night for too long. It seemed that something of their coldness had worked its way into him. He felt chilled and alone, lost. Maybe if he held somebody, a girl, Dark, he'd feel his own warmth again and know for certain who he was. It was possible she felt something similar. He hoped for that too. Certainly, if she turned up unannounced in his room again, he'd be more reluctant to send her away.

Not that the immediate future offered much promise of any kind of one-on-one liaison.

The dozen Bringers and Sicarius himself were seated

on either side of the central cabin of the assault helicopter. Dark was opposite Jake. They all still wore stealth suits. They all carried weapons. They were fast approaching the site identified by Seerborn as the location of IDEA, and they were not expecting the organisation's personnel to welcome them with open arms. 'We have nothing to fear, however,' Sicarius had assured them. 'There will be only a token security presence and before further reinforcements can be summoned a more powerful version of the same device that jammed communications at Deepwater One will isolate the facility from the outside world. The thirteen of us will be more than sufficient to seize the base and finally realise our supreme vision.'

The hatch in the helicopter's floor was open. They had left the arid plain behind them and were now flying over the ruins of an ancient city, cracked pillars of marble, fragments of walls, fallen temples and dismembered statues, pitted and sunken roads leading from desolation to destruction, the desert-bleached bones of a long-dead culture.

Sicarius clapped his hands in delight. 'Ah, the remains of one of my favourite classical civilisations,' he extolled. 'The Euphrasians. Have you heard of the Euphrasians, Dravic?' He hadn't. 'Denver?' Neither had Jake. Sicarius sighed at his own manifest superiority. 'A fine people, the Euphrasians. At their apex, some three thousand years before the birth of Christ, they dominated this region. They believed that the secret of life was to be found in fire and they venerated the power and heat of the earth. Which is why they built Euphrasia, their capital city where they did, close to the volcano their language called Ataposaria or Burning Womb. Sadly for the Euphrasians, Burning Womb gave birth one day. It erupted, buried the city beneath lava and volcanic ash. That was the beginning of the end for the Euphrasians.'

'Like Vesuvius destroying Pompeii.' Jake had enough pride to want to redeem himself. It irked him that a scumbag like Sicarius should know more about stuff than one of the Good Guys.

'An accurate analogy, Jake,' accepted Sicarius. 'Euphrasia lay undiscovered and unknown for centuries until a hundred years ago the excavators and the archaeologists came and went. Too remote an area for tourism. Besides, people these days care only for the pleasure of the present, not the lessons of the past. Now, where once a mighty civilisation flourished, only the scientists of IDEA remain, which seems to me appropriate. Ataposaria laid waste a culture once; though long extinct, it will do so again.'

Jake fought to suppress a shudder. He caught Dark's eye but only briefly as he turned his head to peer out of the window. Ahead, the volcano loomed. Ataposaria. Burning Womb.

Sicarius ordered the pilot to activate the jamming device.

The headquarters of IDEA, particle accelerator and all, were *inside* the volcano.

Jake was in Assault Group A, Dravic commanding. Sicarius himself was leading Assault Group B, which was a downer. Shock blasts tended not to discriminate between enemy and ally; casualties as a result of friendly fire were always a possibility when the shooting started. Jake had hoped to make at least one such occurrence a certainty, but it seemed he was going to be foiled. He'd have to be content with keeping Dark out of harm's way. The Cosmetics Killer was also a member of Assault Group A.

The helicopter had flown above the volcano first. Fifty metres or so below its rim a flat glasteel surface had been constructed extending clear across the crater, like a roof or perhaps a cork in a bottle. Jake had noticed doors set into Ataposaria's wall, like the covering, not the product of nature. Assault Group B would make their entry into IDEA from here.

Their comrades would have a little more work to do.

The tractor beam lowered them to the steep slope of the volcano some eight hundred metres from the complex's main point of ingress, doors that reminded Jake of a giant garage built into the rock. They could have been dropped nearer, but then the chances of being struck by shrapnel would have increased significantly.

Assault Group A found what shelter they could as the helicopter opened fire.

The tactics of the Great War, Jake thought, hugging the ground as if inspired by some amorous intent, keeping his head down. Bludgeon the opposition's trenches with your artillery and pulverise them until all possible resistance must surely have been crushed, then send in the infantry, the soldiers with guns going 'over the top'. A sound enough tactic in theory. The reality, however, lay in the sprawling cemeteries in the Europan districts of France and Belgium, along with the remains of those who'd trusted their generals and died for it.

The assault helicopter's missiles rocked the volcano. Its first sortie demolished the doors, blew them apart, caved them in, crippled whatever defences they might have contained. Its second sent fire and death spouting into the innards of IDEA, an explosive warning for any eager security personnel to keep their distance and, if they wanted to see tomorrow, to drop their weapons. The third sortie, Jake reckoned, as the target area plumed with flame and rubble spat into the air, was for the sheer hell of it.

Dravic was on his feet, yelling something about the glory of Sicarius and the blessing of night. Jake scrambled up too. He could go over the top with the best of them. Maybe this time the tactic would work in practice as well as in theory. It *better* had.

'Come on!' He reached for Dark.

'Hands *off* me!'

So not exactly open-armed forgiveness there, then. But the girl kept close to him as they charged up the incline towards the smoking, blazing gash in the volcano's side. Jake simply hoped she hadn't had the same idea about friendly fire.

The chopper was climbing above Ataposaria, its first task completed. Now it would land Assault Group B on IDEA's roof to create a pincer movement. For that to succeed, those already engaged had to penetrate the facility as promptly and as punishingly as possible.

Dravic was hurling grenades. His fellow Bringers followed suit, sprayed the ruined entranceway with pulse blasts for good measure. Jake did neither. The others were too consumed by righteous rage to notice. Jake was thinking of the controllers at Deepwater One, of Seerborn and anyone else who might have been killed when the bomb went off. He'd be responsible for only one more death on this mission. Then maybe he could find his way back to normal.

Dark was flinging her grenades, but she might as well have been lobbing them in the opposite direction for all the damage they were doing. Jake *wondered*.

And then, with lungs burning and legs aching from their exertions, the Bringers were at the door, what was left of it. Glimpsed through a screen of fire and smoke, a metal corridor, scientific instrumentation that had suffered the computer equivalent of disembowelling, circuitry spilled like intestines, the blur of a white lab coat in flight, several bodies strewn on the floor. Two security men in helmets and uniform down on one knee and preparing to fire. Selecting targets.

Dark.

Jake cannoned into her, his momentum knocking her aside just in time as a pulse blast scorched through the space she'd occupied. They landed heavily but Jake kind of reckoned she'd forgive him that.

It was the final display of defiance from IDEA security at this point. Dravic's pulse blast did *not* miss. The sole remaining defender did not want to litter the floor with his colleagues. Weapon down, arms up. Battle over.

'Denver? Dark?' Dravic almost sounded concerned.

'We're good,' verified Jake.

'Get off me. Get *off*.' Dark rolled out from under him.

'Well pardon me for saving your life.'

Saving life seemed to be the last thing on Dark's mind. Her features contorted as she glared at Jake. 'This means nothing. I owe you *nothing*.'

Jake sat back on his haunches in bewilderment. Behind him, Dravic was laughing.

The surviving security men and the techs had been herded into a storage room and the door sealed. They were irrelevant to Sicarius, beneath his notice. The only members of IDEA's staff who interested him were its project leaders, its scientists, who huddled together before him now in the control centre. There were five of them, three women and two men, all but one clearly over fifty, white-coated and whimpering. Their fear was perhaps unsurprising. A pulse rifle was pointed at each.

'The facility is secure, leader,' reported Dravic.

'Of course,' Sicarius shrugged. 'Did you anticipate any other outcome?'

Jake glowered inwardly. He had an outcome in mind that Sicarius wasn't expecting.

'Professor Takata, I assume that you head the dimensional engineering team.' The terrorist turned his attention to a Japanese woman of about sixty with greying hair and, rather at odds with her colleagues, a resolute expression.

'I do,' the scientist acknowledged, 'though how is it

that a mindless killer such as yourself knows who I am?'

'Professor Takata, please,' protested Sicarius good-humouredly. 'Someone of your intelligence shouldn't fall into the tired trap of equating killing with mindless-ness. Our every action is carried out for a purpose, as you will learn.'

'I'm sorry,' retorted the Professor. 'I mistook you for a terrorist.'

'I am Sicarius and we are the Bringers of the Night.'

Takata seemed taken aback. 'But you can't be. I've seen pictures, news footage . . .'

Sicarius explained. 'You see, I know more about you than you do about me, my dear Professor,' he con-cluded. 'Professor Nagila Takata, until recently Head of Dimensional Engineering at the University of Tokyo, perhaps the world's foremost expert on particle accelera-tion and pioneer of proton conversion. It is an honour to finally meet you. It will be an even greater privilege to work with you.'

'I beg your pardon?'

'Dimensional engineering. That's why we're here. I have some ideas I'd like to try out. Perhaps we could begin by you telling me what stage your own experi-ments have reached.'

'I'll tell you nothing, you monster,' Professor Takata declared.

Sicarius sighed. 'Why must we always go through the same rituals? *Dravic.*'

The lieutenant dutifully raised his shock blaster to Takata's head.

Jake tensed. Acid test. No more corpses on his conscience. If Sicarius ordered Dravic to shoot, he'd get in there first.

'You can kill me if you like.' The Japanese woman had courage all right. 'Though I'll certainly be silent then.'

'Dravic,' said Sicarius, 'kill Professor Takata's colleagues.'

Whimpers became wails. Jake almost swung his pulse rifle round. Only Takata's cry prevented him from betraying himself.

'*Wait!* Wait.'

'Are you feeling more talkative, Professor?' enquired Sicarius.

She told them everything, and everything in the case of the International Dimensional Engineering Agency was incredible to Jake, almost inconceivable. A particle accelerator had been built, for precisely the purpose of colliding protons with antiprotons and thereby generating energy that Sicarius had previously described. It had been built inside the crater of Ataposaria. IDEA's labs, control centre and living quarters clung to the walls of the volcano in several descending circles just below the glasteel roof, as if desiring to keep close to the sky. Much deeper than that, accessed by elevators threaded down the rock-face, was the particle accelerator itself, six storeys high, embedded into the living rock, making of the very crater the circumference of the protons' race-track.

'Come with us, Denver,' Sicarius said. 'You'll want to see this.'

So he travelled down in the elevator with the leader of the Bringers of the Night, with Dravic and with Professor Takata.

Who had already, under duress, activated the accelerator.

Because IDEA had gone further than Jake had imagined, though not far enough for Sicarius. The existence of other dimensions was no longer theory. It was fact. It no longer needed to be proved by mathematics and equations. It could be verified by one's own eyes. Interface had been achieved. The portal had opened.

Jake was about to witness what it disclosed.

Observation level. The small group stepped from the elevator on to a specially insulated floor that was still warm beneath their feet. Not the doing of the volcano. Ataposaria had been extinct for centuries. It was the particle accelerator directly below them that was alive.

Corridor. Was it shaking, just a little, trembling? Or was that Jake himself?

Door. Closed. Maybe for good reason. It would open out on to the crater, the pit, and what could lie out there but a yawning nothingness to the earth's core? Jake wasn't sure he wanted the door to open.

Sicarius *did*. 'Our destiny,' he breathed. Like scripture.

Access mechanism. Pressed. A wondering gasp of air as the door slid aside.

A platform. Beyond it, a bridge like a silver spike.

The party stepped through the doorway.

Jake felt himself groaning, felt a rising sense of

panic, irrational but no less difficult to master because of that.

A sea surged below him, an ocean, a flood. Of deep and unutterable blackness. It was night distilled. It was a world gone blind. It was a coffin buried six feet under. It was all the dark things dreamers dread. And it crashed against the steel walls hooping the crater like ebony surf against the rocks. It was like a beast raging to be free but it was not free. There were lights like beacons set into the walls, dozens of lights braceleting the crater, and the lights burned with stalwart brightness, and though the black mass seethed and heaved, it never rose above them. Jake didn't know what the lights were in scientific terms, but he knew the purpose they served. They were the bars of the cage.

Sicarius made a sound too, one of elation. 'It is true,' he exulted. 'It is *true*.'

And he strode out on to the bridge, the bridge above the darkness, the bridge that spanned the crater. How could he do that? How could he dare?

Jake lurched forward, steadied himself against the guardrail of the platform. He gazed into the blackness beneath. He felt dizzy, unbalanced. It was sucking him in.

'Behold!' Sicarius' voice crackled like lightning. 'The darkness absolute I have promised my believers. The primal darkness. The first night and the last. For there were always two dimensions. Our own false creation of palsied order and sickly light. And *this*, what we see before us now, a dimension of chaos and emptiness and rich, unending dark. Once, long ago, this chaos engulfed our universe too, and covered the earth like a raging ocean.' And as Sicarius threw wide his arms like a worshipper to his god, Jake knew with icy certainty that the terrorist was completely, clinically insane. 'I tell you all,' he howled, 'it will be so once more. The Bringers of the Night will make it so. Chaos and darkness will rise again and *all will die*!'

ELEVEN

They were back in the observation level corridor. Jake was relieved. The swirling darkness of the chaos dimension had affected him almost hypnotically. He felt more in control of himself now, capable of thinking, acting rationally.

The same did not appear to be true for Sicarius.

'The ring of lights, Professor Takata,' he demanded, 'particle inhibitors, yes?' The Japanese woman nodded. 'Then they must be deactivated.'

'No!' As if she was being threatened with murder. 'You can't!'

'Sicarius? Leader?' Dravic would follow the terrorist without demur, but Jake thought he'd feel better if he knew what would happen if the particle inhibitors were deactivated, if the lights went out. In fact, it made him feel worse.

'The inhibitors are the only things keeping the two dimensions apart, Denver,' Sicarius explained tetchily, as if the youth should know. 'They are the dividing line between order and chaos, a line as thin and as fragile as a beam of light. I intend to extinguish that light.'

'But the instability you'll create . . .' Takata was wide-eyed with horror.

'Exactly,' said Sicarius with relish. 'I have done my calculations, Professor. The two dimensions will not be able to exist simultaneously, as night and day cannot occupy the same space at the same time. One must yield to the other, and the energy that produced our universe is already in decline. It will not be able to resist the strength and power of chaos.'

'So what's,' Jake ventured nervously, 'going to, like, happen?'

'Darkness will spout from this volcano and crack the earth in two. It will gather in the skies, it will pour into the skies like black blood. It will engulf the world and bring upon us the blessing of eternal night. *Apocalypse.*' Sicarius whispered the word like the name of his true love. 'A glorious return to the first day – minus one.'

'I'll not help you.' Takata was adamant. 'Kill me. Kill the others. We're not important.'

'Correct,' said Sicarius. 'You are not important, but then neither are any of us. Only the cause matters, the bringing of the night. My task will soon be done and I will be fulfilled. You will live to witness, Takata, but I no longer need you. I can initiate the inhibitors' deactivation sequence myself. Please.' He indicated the elevator. 'Shall we?'

'Sicarius, you mustn't do this.' A final, feeble protest from the Professor. 'It'll mean the end of everything.'

'I know,' said Sicarius. And smiled.

Jake strode to the control centre with a purposefulness on the brink of panic. Part of him was screaming that he should run, but another part feared that if he started to run, he might not stop, that he'd race out of the complex, down the side of the volcano, and maybe have reached the ruins of Euphrasia before chaos unleashed flooded over him and turned everything black. Panic wasn't an option. He had to keep order in his mind. Given the awesome scale of the threat he faced, however, it wasn't easy, despite his training. He thought ruefully of the Deveraux motto: 'Keeping the world safe for tomorrow'. Right now, keeping the world *alive* for tomorrow would be a major achievement.

Dark was among the Bringers in the control centre. Good. 'We need to talk,' he told her urgently.

'You might need to,' Dark said scornfully. 'I—'

'Not here.' He grabbed her arm as discreetly as was possible and pulled her towards the door.

'What do you think you're doing?' the girl hissed, but she went with him, and she didn't call out to the others. She let herself be led into a side-corridor before she spoke up again. 'Now do you mind explaining yourself? You needn't think you can get back in with me just because of what happened before. You had your chance and you—'

'Shut up, Dark.'

'What?' Surprised by the gravity of Jake's tone.

'This isn't about you and me. It's about . . . more than that. Listen, I'm taking a chance just telling you this, but I don't reckon anyone's taken a chance on you before, have they, Dark?'

She ignored the question. 'Telling me what?'

'You've got to get out of here.'

Dark scowled, baffled. 'What are you *talking* about?'

He was grabbing her arm again, squeezing. 'Do you know what Sicarius is *doing* here?'

'I guess we're gonna blow the place up, make a big bang.'

'Big Bang is right.' Jake smiled thinly. 'This organisation, IDEA, it's opened a portal to another dimension, a chaos dimension.'

'Jake, I never went to school after sixth grade. If that means anything, you'd better just tell me what.'

'Darkness and death, that's what it means.'

'What I said. We're gonna blow the place up.'

'The world, Dark.' His other hand. Her other arm. 'The place he's gonna destroy is the whole damn *world*.'

'You're kidding me. That's impossible, right?' She wanted to scoff. She wanted her tone to express ridicule. But when she looked into Jake's burning eyes she couldn't manage either.

'Sicarius is mad, Dark. He's in love with death.'

'You'd better be careful what you're saying, Jake. If Sicarius heard you talking about him like that—'

'He's got to be stopped.'

'Will you stop talking like that? You keep on talking like that and I'll have to tell Sicarius and then where will you be?'

'I can't let it happen, Dark. I won't. I want you to leave before I make my move.'

'I can't do that. You mustn't say that. You're not one of us when you do. You're a traitor.'

'You're not the same as the others either, Dark. You know you're not.'

'I am.'

'You're not. Your blaster never jammed before, did it? You just couldn't bring yourself to use it.'

'I belong here.'

'You don't. Now's your chance to get out. Go.'

'*Go where*, Jake?' Dark's green eyes desperate, lost, hurt. 'Go *where*? Tell me. Tell me where someone like me can go. I've *done* things, Jake, I've done terrible things, and they make me the same as Sicarius, they *do*, they mark me out. That's why I have to stay with the Bringers. There's no way back for me, no way out. I *belong* to them. Where can I go where my crimes won't follow me and track me down? Who's ever going to forgive me?'

'I am.' Jake's voice was decisive and sincere. 'I forgive you, Dark. And I want you to live, but to do that you have to leave, *now*. Because if you stay here, Sicarius will destroy you.'

She shook herself free of him. She was mournful, even pitiful. 'I can't. I don't have the strength. I'm sorry.'

She ran.

'Dark, wait!'

Jake called after her, and he longed to chase after her too, but he didn't dare. The mission. In the field, only the mission mattered. Possibly he'd jeopardised it already by revealing his intention to Dark. What if she was sprinting straight to Sicarius? What if her loyalties truly lay with the terrorists? Jake might just have endangered the future of the world for the sake of a single girl, and not exactly a spotless innocent, either. It wasn't what his old teachers would have called playing the mission percentages. It wasn't professional. But somehow he couldn't bring himself to feel bad about it. Dark deserved a second chance. Everyone did.

Jake's expression hardened. Everyone except Sicarius.

So he had to move quickly. Roll-call. Dravic: escorting Professor Takata to confinement in the storage room with her erstwhile colleagues. Sicarius himself: commencing the arduous process of hacking into IDEA's mainframe and gleaning from it the inhibitor deactivation sequence. Jake hadn't actually heard the terrorist use the word 'arduous'. That was wishful thinking on his own part. Because if IDEA's systems were easy to infiltrate, or if Sicarius turned out to be a hacker supreme, like Cally at the top of her game, then whatever Jake did now probably wouldn't matter.

But Jake couldn't accept that. He'd make it matter.

He made swift progress to the communications room. The systems that had been jammed for the attack were up and running again now, Sicarius hinting something about a final broadcast to the world before night fell. Jake was grateful to the Bringer for once. He intended to make a little broadcast of his own first. The mission had grown too big. There were too many variables. An agent in his situation couldn't afford to be proud. It was time to summon reinforcements.

Dravic stood between him and the comlinks. 'What do you want, Denver?' He must have secured Takata with record speed. He regarded Jake curiously. At least he evidently hadn't also been talking with Dark.

'Ah, Sicarius,' Jake improvised. 'He sent me, instructed me to help you out. Ah, here. In communications.'

Improvised weakly. An unlikely order, given that three Bringers besides Dravic were currently occupied monitoring screens linked to hidden surveillance cameras in the surrounding area.

It didn't look like he was fooling Dravic. The terrorist's naturally angular face grew sharper still, like a knife being whetted. 'Are you sure?' he said. 'We already seem to have more than our necessary complement of volunteers.'

'Well, yeah, but that's what he said. If you want to check' – indicating the comlink – 'but I don't reckon he'll appreciate the interruption.'

It was a gamble. If Dravic decided to believe him, or at least not to risk Sicarius' wrath, he'd be able to transmit his Deveraux distress code without too much trouble. If the terrorist opted to comlink Sicarius, however . . .

Jake weighed up his chances of taking out all four Bringers in an enclosed space without sustaining serious injury. It wasn't surprising that secret agents found life insurance hard to come by.

Dravic glanced to the comlink. 'Perhaps I'd better . . .'

Jake steadied himself. Dravic was the main threat. Remove Dravic first. Remove him —

'Dravic!' One of the Bringers at the screens. 'Look!'

He did. The screen in question displayed part of the ruined city and, just at the moment, something else as well. Dravic's eyes narrowed. 'It seems we have unexpected visitors. Well, they must be provided for.' The Bringer at the console appeared puzzled. 'We have an assault helicopter idling on the roof, do we not? Let us welcome our guests as our glorious leader would wish. Let us bestow the blessing of the night upon them.'

And Jake was watching the screen now too, and his mind was racing.

The terrorists saw only two girls in silver suits on SkyBikes skimming above the jagged surface of Euphrasia, one girl with blonde hair, one girl with blue. Jake saw more than that.

Seemed something of a Bond Team reunion was on the cards.

'Where would we be without the Deveraux travel service?' said Bex.

'Somewhere that's alive, maybe.' Lori studied the shattered city with distaste. 'Somewhere that isn't horizon-to-horizon desolation and decay.'

'Okay, so New York City is out. But what I really mean is, if it wasn't for Dad's worldwide network of transport options we could never have got this close to IDEA this quickly. Just let the techs read our bio-signature and the world's our oyster, no questions asked. Which given why we're here is a bit of a bonus, wouldn't you say?' Bex sighed, aware that her companion had hardly listened to a single word. 'Hey, Lori? *Lo.*'

'Hmm?' Lori was thinking that this city must have been beautiful once, a testament to Mankind's creativity and ingenuity, a spectacle of soaring temples and noble statues in marble and bronze, a haven of light and hope. And now all was fallen, dreams dashed, lives forgotten. Why did good things have to end? Why could nothing precious last?

Lori was thinking, *Jake.*

'It's going to be all right, Lo,' Bex assured her as friends do when the opposite might just as easily be the case. 'We'll get to Jake. Thanks to Professor Seerborn.'

'It felt bad running off and leaving him, Bex.' Lori winced at the memory, vacating the Professor's study and retreating to their one half-crippled SkyBike with the old man still in his chair.

'Yeah, but you know we couldn't stay,' Bex said. 'Spy High operatives don't do explanations. Anyway, the medtechs I bet looked after him better than we could have done.'

'Do you think he told the authorities what he told us?'

Bex doubted it. 'If he did, surely we'd have been rubbing shoulders with the official security agencies by now, and I can't even see a guy with a beard and a spade digging up bits of old pottery. Nah, poor old fellow was losing it before we left. Shock. Post-traumatic stress. All that not-coping stuff. Wouldn't have made much sense. It's down to us to stop Null.'

'Us and Jake,' Lori corrected.

'Yeah. Us and Jake.'

Lori scanned all around her, the crumbled city silent but for the reverberation of the SkyBikes' propulsion units, the volcano towering grand and aloof in the distance. 'But what if Seerborn was wrong, Bex, and we're on some kind of wild-goose chase.'

'Wild? Geese'd be furious out in this heat.'

'Be *serious*, Bex. I can't see any sign of scientists or terrorists or anyone.'

'Then let's hope they can't see us, either,' Bex remarked.

But though both girls' senses and observational skills were hypersensitive after years of training at Spy High, travelling as quickly over the broken terrain as they were, even they could not assimilate every single detail. The occasional decapitated marble head, for example, curly-haired, often bearded, always proud despite the fact that it had lain in the dust for centuries. The occasional head whose eyes actually moved, almost as if the original sightless stone had recently been replaced by something more modern, eyes that seemed to be constantly, restlessly roaming, perhaps in search of the body from which they were once so rudely parted. Or perhaps not. For the moment, at least, they seemed more interested in the two newcomers on SkyBikes.

And the volcano loomed closer all the time.

'Lori, isn't that some kind of entrance up there, below the rim?' Bex pointed.

'*Was*, more like.' Lori saw the doorway to IDEA for

the first time. 'Looks like someone huffed and puffed, terrorist style.'

'Score one for Professor Seerborn,' said Bex. 'Ah, and Lo? Do you hear that kind of buzzing?'

Lori lifted her gaze higher still. 'Here comes the wolf.'

Assault helicopter. Rising apparently from within the volcano, streaking towards them with single-minded intent, zeroing in.

'Is it me,' Bex wondered, 'or does this guy not look friendly?'

Flares from the chopper's missile launchers, like matches being lit. The scream of approaching death through the air.

'Whatever gave you that idea?' said Lori. '*Evasive.*'

The ground ahead of them erupted in fire and rock.

'You're right, Dravic,' he admitted, backing towards the door, 'you don't need me here.'

The terrorist was paying no attention, too busy com-linking the helicopter's pilot. 'I want that bird in the air now!'

'Maybe I'll just kind of reassign myself.' Easing out of the communications room.

And hurtling for the roof. The chopper wasn't taking off without him.

The adrenalin pumped through Jake's body, invigorating him. At last it seemed his pretence could end. At last he could be himself, no longer Jake Denver but Jake Black.

But what were Lori and Bex doing here? Were they somehow also assigned to bringing down Sicarius? How could they know that Sicarius was here? Or IDEA? Or Jake himself? Had they somehow learned about the Black Ops division? Was this to do with him more than the Bringers of the Night?

Jake burst out on to the roof. At the present moment, it was doubling as a helipad.

And keep the questions for later. The helicopter's rotors were beginning to turn.

Pound those legs. Strain those muscles. *Sprint.*

The chopper was trembling in take-off.

The side doors were open. Sometimes luck was on the side of the Good Guys. Fifty metres to go.

He'd been told once, you should never approach a helicopter from behind. The rear rotor blades were too dangerous. Jake had never been afraid of a bit of danger. Their razor whirl was in his ears, their steel blur in his sight. He'd also seen an old movie once where a guy had had the top of his head sliced clean off by a helicopter rotor blade.

Not him, though. Not today.

Jake dived into the central cabin, collided with its unyielding metal floor, rolled. Bruises weren't important. Timing was. And his had been perfect. The chopper was in the air and if he'd been three seconds later he'd never have made it.

He was aboard. Good. *Unseen.* Better. A moment to gather his wits and then he might just have a quiet word with the occupants of the cockpit.

The city of Euphrasia had suffered greater devastation than this in its long, chequered past. Not much could equal the eruption of Ataposaria three millennia ago, certainly not the ravages of a single assault helicopter.

Truth to tell, though, that wasn't much of a consolation for Lori and Bex.

Their SkyBikes sped above what must once have been a broad, dignified avenue. Missile to the right, obliterating what was left of a wall, spraying masonry at Bex and causing her to yelp as sharp fragments of debris pinged against the chassis of her bike and tore at her leg. Missile to the left, skittling columns of long-lost temples, crashing them down in thunderous blocks in Lori's path, testing her sky-biking skills to their limit. Missile ahead, uprooting the avenue and hurling its weathered brick at the two girls with all the eagerness of a mob stoning a scarlet woman in less enlightened times.

'He's finding his range!' Bex yelled. 'Split!'

Lori nodded. 'Good luck!' she cried, veering left, though possibly she had the more pressing need for fortune.

The helicopter chose to bear down on her.

When the missiles started firing, Jake decided he should start moving. Drawing his shock blaster, he opened the cockpit door.

'Room for one more?'

Pilot and co-pilot, right and left. Pilot simply astonished by Denver's sudden appearance with a blaster bared for action. Co-pilot quicker off the mark, quicker to act. Too quick, in fact.

His jabbing elbow caught Jake in a tender spot that would have earned disqualification in a boxing match.

No referee on board assault helicopters as a rule, however. And no rules, either.

Jake staggered back, struck the cockpit's rear wall. The co-pilot was lunging from his chair. Sitting down he'd looked normal. Standing up he looked huge. Could probably get his fist entirely round Jake's head and *squeeze*. A shock blast, though, was no respecter of size. Window of opportunity.

'Sicarius One to control.' Pilot on the comlink. 'We —'

Couldn't let him make that call. Jake fired his blaster all right, but at the comlink panel rather than the co-pilot. The former exploded in sparks. The latter bulldozed into Jake.

A meaty hand clamped around the teenager's throat. He'd been right about the squeezing. The co-pilot's other hand performed the same function on Jake's wrist, forcing him to drop the shock blaster. Jake pummelled at his assailant's midriff, or where he supposed the man's midriff to be. He seemed more like one solid mass of muscle. His blows made no impact.

'You're tickling,' grinned the co-pilot.

In a lighter moment, Jake might have asked which gym the big man attended. But as the choking pressure on his windpipe increased, his situation was only getting darker.

The rain of missiles had ceased. Maybe they'd all been used up. Maybe the pilot had thought better of ruthlessly targeting an almost defenceless girl. Lori sometimes had such an improving effect on men.

Or maybe he was simply switching to a different kind of weaponry.

The metallic rattle of automatic gunfire lacerated the sky. Shells ripped through the ancient marble of Euphrasia, stitching a deadly pattern in the direction of Lori.

She accelerated again, but how long could this chase last? Hunter and hunted, someone had to win in the end, and Lori was sick of playing the quarry. Her bike boasted weapons systems too. If she could only engineer an opening for them. No good expecting her pursuer to pause while she set herself up for a counter-attack. She'd have to manoeuvre sharply, suddenly, decisively.

Without even a thought of reducing speed, Lori swung her SkyBike violently, precipitately into a U-turn.

And the tactic was likely to prove decisive, sure. But not as the blonde girl had hoped. The bike's forward momentum was too great for it to obey its rider. Its propulsion units screeched in protest. The entire machine was thrown wildly into the SkyBike equivalent of a skid.

Lori cried out as she realised the mistake she'd made, but she couldn't repair it. Height lost. Collision with ground assured. She threw herself out of the saddle before impact. Finding herself trapped under a SkyBike with a broken leg was not conducive to her continued survival.

Slamming to the ground but using her training to alleviate the chances of crippling herself was better. Potentially better. Bleeding from her lip, battered until much of her body was probably as blue as Bex's hair, Lori at least had the comfort that her limbs were essentially intact. She struggled to stand on two of them.

Yeah. *Potentially* better.

Spitting pellets of fire, the assault helicopter closed in for the kill.

'Time to embrace the night, traitor,' leered the co-pilot.

Jake squirmed but he was beginning to understand what a fish on a hook must feel like. Unless the big man for some reason relaxed his grip, he was finished. He thought he could hear machine-gun fire. Lori. Bex. He couldn't let them down.

The co-pilot was drawing back his boulder of a fist. He was pinning Jake to the wall with his other hand, throttling him, a process that while pleasurable to the one inflicting it was proving too slow. The fist would bring matters to a more immediate conclusion.

Jake saw his chance. The cockpit door was still open. He lifted his legs, the pressure from his assailant preventing him from falling, jammed his boots against the inside of the doorway – here came the fist like a missile of flesh and bone – and *pushed*. Pushed hard.

His body slid along the wall scarcely a foot. But it was enough. Instead of the sound of fist on face like meat slapped on to a slab, the more metallic thud of fingers cracking against steel.

The co-pilot bellowed. His unbroken fingers quivered in sympathy with their brethren.

Jake was free.

And dropping low. The co-pilot had a lot of weight. It could be turned against him. Jake scythed the man's legs with one of his own. Didn't wait for gravity. Gave it not so much a helping hand as a helping barrage of double-fisted blows.

With a disbelieving groan, the big man collapsed across the lap of the helicopter's pilot. 'What are you —'

Ejector seat control. 'Looks like you've got to fly,' quipped Jake. And pressed it.

Lori set her shock blaster to Materials. She'd never shot down an enemy assault helicopter this way before but there was a first time for everything. There'd *better* be.

But suddenly the chopper wasn't spewing bullets any more. And suddenly the pilot's ejector hatch had blown and two guys on one chair were sailing through the air, the seat's parachute opening as it should.

Hmm.

Co-pilot's hatch the same. Co-pilot's chair. The more traditional single occupant. A younger guy. Black hair.

'Hah!' Lori shouted her delight. She ignored her pain. She ignored the helicopter careering over her head and crashing to the ground way behind her. She ran towards its last evacuee's landing point.

She very much wanted to throw her arms around Jake.

'Sleeping like babies,' Bex reported of the pilot and co-pilot, tapping her wristband as if that might have had something to do with it. 'Pretty ugly babies, mind, but there'll be no more trouble from them.'

'That's good,' Jake said tersely. 'We'll get enough of that from Dravic and Sicarius.'

'And Null?' Lori suggested.

'Lo, Null *is* Sicarius. The Sicarius the public sees is a hologram.'

'Terrorists aren't the only ones appearing under false pretences,' Bex observed. Now that their initial hugs and greetings were over, the initial thrill of their reunion, she felt it was time to get down to business. 'We know about the Black Ops, Jake. We know about the staged mind-wipe and the animate working your dad's fields. We know about Jake Black.'

Jake nodded. 'I guessed as much when I saw you on the bikes,' he said. He wasn't sure whether he was happy or horrified. He supposed it depended on how the knowledge would change his relationship with his former partners. 'Did Deveraux send you?'

'My esteemed father doesn't know we know,' Bex said. 'Neither does anyone else.'

'Then why are you both here?'

'We came to stop you, Jake.'

Lori's eyes were candid and searching. Jake couldn't meet their gaze. 'From what?' He knew.

'From killing Sicarius. From *killing* anyone.'

He shook his head wearily. 'We've been through this before, Lo. You know how I feel. I'm sure Bex does, too. And I'm not bound by Spy High rules any more. I'm not a teeny playing at secret agents.'

'Playing at judge, jury and executioner suit you better, Jake?' Bex said.

'Valuing life, Jake, it's not about rules, it's about the

kind of person you want to be, it's about being at peace with yourself.' Lori tried to put her arms around him. His muscles were tensed and tight.

'Will you let go?' He didn't want anyone close to him right now, including Lori. *Especially* Lori. 'I'm perfectly happy with the way I am, thanks.'

'You kill, Jake, and you step into the abyss.'

'Thanks a lot for the sermon, Reverend Angel, but do you think we can bypass the collection and the hymns and get straight to the part where the congregation saves the planet from certain death? 'Cause if we don't put Sicarius out of commission pronto, he's gonna be bringing the abyss to *us*.'

Dravic had patched the feed from the surveillance cameras through to the control centre. One by one, however, their hidden eyes had been inadvertently blinded by the assault helicopter's weaponry. He and Sicarius now watched as the final camera transmitted trembling pictures of the chopper plummeting from the sky directly at it.

'If only we'd seen more clearly what happened,' Dravic bemoaned. 'Garrett tried to tell us something but then the comlink shut off. Systems failure, do you think, leader? Sabotage?'

They'd have had a clearer idea if the last camera had been situated in such a position as to witness the ejections from the helicopter. Luckily for the Deveraux agents but unluckily for the Bringers of the Night, this had not been the case.

Sicarius did not seem to care. 'Treachery from within

our own number, Dravic? Unlikely. But even if so, and even if the female intruders have survived our airborne attack, our enemies will remain unable to check the advance of night. The final inhibitor deactivation codes have been confirmed. We can begin the sequence immediately. Rejoice, my faithful one. This wretched world has less than an hour to live.'

TWELVE

There was a hole in the side of the volcano where the entrance to IDEA had used to be. It was guarded by two Bringers of the Night.

'Denver?' queried the first, though she'd seen him often enough before. It was the two teenaged girls with him she didn't recognise, the girls in silver who trudged ahead of her fellow terrorist in the manner of captives.

'Prisoners,' Jake confirmed. 'I'm taking them to Sicarius.'

'We saw the helicopter fly,' said the second Bringer. 'We saw it fall. If these unbelievers are responsible they should die now.'

'Thing is,' said Jake, 'they *weren't* responsible. I was.'

He was responsible for flooring the second Bringer with a well-placed stun blast as well. The man's comrade began to raise her own weapon but it hadn't exceeded hip height before Lori's boot sent it spinning from her hand in a crackle of sparks. She and Bex had energised their shock-suits. Lori followed up with a combination of blows, each one flashing like neon, which quickly rendered the first Bringer as unconscious as her partner.

'I'll just take a seat while you two do all the work, shall I?' said Bex.

'There are terrorists to go round,' Jake replied tersely. 'Ten of them, including Sicarius.' He almost excluded Dark from the count. He *wanted* to, but after their parting exchange knew that he didn't dare. To make unfounded assumptions about Dark's loyalties could place Lori and Bex in danger.

'So let's jump to the "and then there were none" part,' urged Bex. 'Which way are we going?'

'Control centre.'

For a Deveraux agent, to reach a decision and to act on it was the same thing. Jake led his team-mates racing through the corridors, Bex to his left, Lori to his right. The blonde girl glanced at her former boyfriend, tried to interpret his state of mind from his expression. Difficult. Jake's features were closed and fixed with absolute concentration, but inside he had to be in turmoil. Had she and Bex found him in time or had the decision to kill already been made?

Control centre, up ahead. Door closed. A single terrorist on guard.

Bex's sleepshot reduced their adversaries to single figures. 'Now I feel I've contributed,' she commented with satisfaction.

'Door?' said Lori.

'Not for long.' Jake flipped his blaster to Materials, fired.

In the headquarters of the International Dimensional

Engineering Agency, the practice of replacing entrances with holes seemed to be catching on.

Three on three, and the Spy High graduates had not been startled by the explosion at the door. Lori and Bex eliminated the Bringers at the control centre's consoles with sleepshot. Jake did *not* open fire on Dravic, but only a monumental exercise of willpower was keeping his trigger finger under control.

The terrorist raised empty hands. For a man in the act of surrendering, however, he looked pretty pleased with himself.

'I assume this means you're a traitor, Denver,' Dravic observed.

'You're the traitor, scumbag,' Jake spat, 'to the whole human race. Where's Sicarius?'

'You're too late,' Dravic smiled. 'The deactivation sequence has already begun. The countdown to chaos is underway. Night comes, children. Fear it.'

'Yeah? Well you won't be around to see it, Dravic.'

'Jake!' Lori saw what he was about to do, couldn't stop him from doing it.

The blast knocked Dravic off his feet.

'No!' He'd killed the terrorist. She was sickeningly sure of it. She darted to the fallen man's side.

'What are you wasting your time on filth like Dravic for, Lo?' Jake sounded offended. 'He's the guy ending the world, remember? And if you're interested, my blaster's set back on Stun.'

'But why shoot at all, Jake?' Bex criticised. 'We might have needed this guy.'

'We don't. We never would.' Jake was like steel.

'Here's how we save the planet. You two go up one level. You saw the stairwell from the corridor. Storage rooms. That's where IDEA's scientists are being held. Free them. Tell Professor Takata Sicarius has started deactivating the particle inhibitors. She's got to reverse the process.'

'What if she can't?' said Bex.

'Lights out.'

'Then let's hope she can. *Lori.*' Moving to the doorway.

'Jake, what are you going to do?' Lori wasn't quite as ready to depart.

'I'm going after Sicarius.'

'But you didn't give Dravic the chance to tell you where—'

'I know where he is, Lori,' Jake gritted.

'And when you find him, Jake,' Lori pressed, 'what are you going to do *then*?'

It was a question to which he had no answer.

The elevator plunged him to the observation level. If Sicarius had been wearing a homing device, Jake couldn't have been more certain of the terrorist's location. He was on the bridge above the pit. He was watching the blackness grow. He wasn't hiding or running or trying to escape. He was embracing the darkness, before the darkness embraced him.

Jake planned on getting there first.

Was it his imagination, or was the light in the elevator flickering, as if about to be extinguished? Problem with the generators, perhaps. And where did Lori get off with this whole moral conscience thing? Who appointed her his Jiminy Cricket? He didn't need her, those blue eyes kind of challenging him, reminding him of feelings it was safer to ignore. He was Black Ops now. Jake Black. He could do whatever was necessary to complete his mission, Jonathan Deveraux had said it himself, anything and everything. Guilt-free. What did Lori know about Sicarius, what he'd done, what he was capable of doing? Only Jake knew. Only Jake could put an end to it.

He was lying on the floor before the doors slid open. Two more of Sicarius' followers, eyes trained five to six feet higher than that. Stun blasts removed them from his path. No obstacles now. Through the door, beyond the platform, Sicarius was waiting, waiting for Jake to join him, the teenager somehow sensed.

He was on his feet again. He was darting forward.

'Jake!'

Careless. He whirled towards the sound of the voice. So fixated on Sicarius, he hadn't checked that no more Bringers were loitering with intent in the immediate vicinity. One was. Good job it was only Dark.

Dark with shock blaster. Barrel pointing unmissably at his chest.

She'd been too reckless. They both had, attacking the Bringers outside the storage room without considering the advantage offered by even modest cover. At Deveraux they'd been taught never to neglect the basics, no matter how desperate the situation. Circumstances would not be improved by an agent throwing his or her life away needlessly. Bex guessed that in some matters, at least, her father was always right.

But the gash in her arm wasn't so bad. The contrast of red blood against silver shock-suit made the wound look worse than it was. That was what she told Lori, in any case.

'Are you sure?' The blonde girl had survived the skirmish predictably unblemished.

'Lori, if we don't move it won't matter one way or the other.'

Lori nodded. She stepped over the insensate bodies of the two Bringer guards. The Materials setting of her shock blaster burst open the storage door.

Inside, frightened men and women in white coats cowered against the walls. Only one person stood defiant, a grey-haired Japanese woman.

'Professor Takata,' Lori said. 'We need you.'

'You gonna shoot me, Dark?' It was almost a dare.

'The leader's orders,' Dark said. 'Anybody tries to get to him, make sure they don't.'

'You could do it,' Jake admitted. 'I'm fast, but maybe not *that* fast. And you'll *have* to do it, Dark, 'cause I can't stop now. But the big question is, do you *want* to do it? You want to follow Sicarius to the death? That's the only place he's leading you. There's not a "sic" in his name for nothing. Tell me that's what you really want.' His eyes met hers, held hers. 'It's make a choice time, Dark.'

And he was ready for either. He *was* fast. The moment it looked like she was going to fire he'd be leaping forward.

'Jake . . .'

What happened next was down to Dark.

'You're right.' She lowered her blaster, lowered her eyes. 'I can't do it. I don't want to.'

'That's good, Dark.'

'I don't want to die. I want to live.'

'That's good.'

Jake smiled. He very much wanted to hold her. Could be the final tender moment before the end of the world.

'Sicarius has locked himself inside the crater, Jake. You'll have to blast the door.'

That was the trouble with tender moments in the secret agent business, however. There was always violence to be done first.

Violence and death and an endless queue of madmen. The ingredients of Jake's life. He was no longer smiling. His expression darkened. 'No problem.'

He blasted the door as if it had caused him personal affront, but it was evidently made of sterner stuff than its counterpart at the control centre. The metal was dented and blackened, but it did not yield.

'Dark,' snapped Jake, 'join your fire with mine. Quickly!'

The girl obeyed. Twin shock blasts shook the door, reverberated through the corridor. The metal was buckling, bending. 'Again!' Flames flared. Smoke billowed. Electronics erupted. 'Again! Again!' A rhythm of destruction. And Jake wasn't seeing the door now, an inanimate hulk of metal. He was seeing Averill Frankenstein and Talon and Vlad Tepesch and Alexander Cain and Mickey Lorenzo, all the lunatics he'd fought in his time at Spy High, and they were all

cohering, combining, and all of them were Sicarius.
'Again!' The blaster was hot in his hand.

'Jake, stop! You don't . . .' Dark hanging on his arm.
'Stop. It's done.'

'What?' He could hardly bring himself to cease shooting. It seemed easier just to continue. Maybe in a
moment. And Dark was right: they'd finally forced a
jagged, smouldering breach in the door. Maybe once he'd
stepped through it.

And Lori wasn't around. That was just as well.

'Wait for me here,' Jake told Dark.

Lori wouldn't want to see what he was going to do to
Sicarius.

Professor Nagila Takata was unaccustomed to vigorous
physical exercise. By the time she'd returned to the
control centre with her strange liberators and her colleagues she was wheezing badly, but this was no
occasion to saunter or stroll. At least her mind could race
more effectively than her body.

She sat at her computer, brought up the details of the
inhibitor deactivation sequence. Her spontaneous frown
did not inspire Lori and Bex to a joyful embrace. 'The
sequence is already considerably advanced,' the
Professor said.

'Can you stop it, though?' Bex rephrased for greater
positivity. 'I mean, you can stop it, though, right?'

'If anybody can, I can,' said Professor Takata,
which, while free of false modesty, as a declaration still
lacked the absolute certainty that Bex had been hoping
for.

'Are we working to a deadline here?' Lori sought to clarify.

'If I haven't arrested the process in five minutes,' the Japanese woman predicted, activating a viewing screen, 'our universe will be inundated with *this*.'

Inside the particle accelerator. Lori and Bex for the first time saw the tide of blackness crashing against the walls, kept at bay by the light of the inhibitors. For the first time they saw the glittering ribbon of the bridge spanning the turmoil. A lone man was using that vantage point to admire the view, his hands clasped leisurely behind his back.

'Null,' Lori said.

'Sicarius,' Bex corrected.

And somebody else, entering through a rent in the wall, advancing purposefully on to the platform, somebody Lori could not mistake. 'Jake,' she breathed.

The explosions bombarding the door had informed Sicarius of an enemy's approach. Jake's appearance added its identity.

'Denver! Jake!' he hailed from the bridge. 'Have you come for your front-row seat to Armageddon?'

'Not quite, scumbag,' Jake glowered. 'I've come for you.'

Sicarius shook his head and tutted. 'I'm disappointed in you, Jake. I expected better, a young man of your evident intelligence. And working for some lamentable security agency as well, I assume. Surely you ought to be welcoming the blessing of the night with the proverbial open arms.'

'What are you talking about?'

'Your motivation, Jake. I understand you. You are angered by the existence of evil in the world, are you not? Your nice, tidy little concept of evil. You want to defeat it, remove it, to make the world a better place. I understand that.' Sicarius chuckled tolerantly. 'And darkness can achieve it. When the inhibitors fail and the chaos dimension is unleashed, night will cover the earth and there will be no more evil. Surely this is an outcome your painfully conventional principles should applaud?'

'Yeah? But there'll be no more good either, no more life.' Jake felt rage rising within him as the blackness boiled in the pit.

'You can't make an omelette without breaking a few eggs,' shrugged Sicarius.

'Your logic's as twisted as your mind, you murdering scum.'

'Ah, name-calling. The final refuge of the intellectually bereft.' Sicarius sighed. 'So even though your cause is hopeless, Jake, you still oppose me.'

'Is the night dark?'

'Then you give me no choice.'

The terrorist moved with surprising speed. His hands were no longer behind his back. One of them was holding a shock blaster.

The first shot struck the platform's guardrail, like a firework detonating before Jake's eyes. The second hit the wall behind him as he ducked, crouched, returned fire.

Then several things seemed to happen at once.

Sicarius crying out in pain, clutching his bloodied

hand to him. His shock blaster spinning through the air, dropping through the dimming light of the inhibitors and swallowed by the surging maelstrom beneath like a stone thrown into dark waters. Sicarius staggering backwards, toppling, a diver with no sense of technique.

Jake running, darting forward, abandoning the relative solidity of the platform for the more tenuous support of the bridge. His booted feet clattering.

Had he intended only to disarm Sicarius? Or had he meant to kill? Had his shot been perfect or poor?

The bridge seemed to be swaying. The yawning gulf of blackness beckoned.

Sicarius slipping over the edge. Jake lunging, groping, grasping.

He was on his knees, perilously perched above the pit, but he had hold of the terrorist's uninjured arm. The leader of the Bringers of the Night dangled helplessly between dimensions.

Sicarius' life was in Jake's hands – literally.

'Ah, Jake, how history repeats itself.' For a man on the brink of a fatal plunge, Sicarius was remarkably philosophical. 'I save you on the bridge at Deepwater One. Now comes your chance to return the favour.'

Jake's laugh was brief and bitter. 'Sicarius, what makes you think I'm gonna save you?'

Professor Takata shouted. No words, just noise. Bex wasn't sure whether that meant the world was doomed or whether it had narrowly earned a reprieve. She was kind of praying for the latter.

'That's it!' the Japanese woman exulted. 'Inhibitor deactivation sequence halted. Reversal of sequence commenced.'

'That's *it*?' Bex was cautious of happy endings. 'So you're saying danger's over? I can go ahead and book next year's holiday?'

'That's the good news,' said Professor Takata.

'Don't tell me. This whole facility, on the other hand, is gonna blow inside a minute.'

'Not quite,' dismissed Takata, 'but the partial deactivation has produced significant pressure at the dimensional interface.'

'I knew it,' groaned Bex. 'What are those dimensional interfaces *like*? Lori, are you listening to this?'

Scarcely. The blonde girl was transfixed by the viewing screen of the particle accelerator. It wasn't pleasant to watch someone you cared for under fire.

'Lori, Jake can look after *himself*.' Had to, Bex reasoned. *Was* doing, as he shot back at Sicarius. The girls' priority was to protect the scientist while she saved lives. 'Professor Takata?'

'The pressure needs to be released. The system has what you might call an inbuilt safety valve. In short, a single escape of other-dimensional material is inevitable.'

'An explosion, right?'

'Jake,' Lori whispered as her former boyfriend charged on to the bridge.

'An explosion, very possibly,' Professor Takata conceded. 'We shouldn't be harmed here, but anybody still inside the crater —'

'*Jake.*' Lori was already on her way.

'Lo, wait!' Unheeded. Bex turned back to Takata. 'How long?'

'If I were you I wouldn't go anywhere near the particle accelerator.'

'If I were *you*, Professor,' Bex responded, 'neither would I. Unfortunately . . .' It appeared the Deveraux agent had a new priority. 'Keep working. We'll be back.' And she was off and running. 'Lori, I meant wait for *me* . . .'

The darkness swilled beneath them. It seemed to Jake as if it was reaching for them with inchoate black fingers, seeking to seize Sicarius, seize Jake himself, drag them down into the void. The darkness seemed to be thriving, swelling, as if it was feeding off something, leeching a kind of life. It had a sound like thunder rolling in across barren hills, like the wind across the moors at midnight.

It was difficult to concentrate.

'Sicarius, what makes you think I'm gonna save you?'

'What otherwise was the purpose of your theatrical heroics?' The hanging man's expression exhibited only contempt. 'Why risk your own safety to grab my arm? Your miserably predictable code of false ethics. I could have killed your mother and you'd still try to save me.'

'Don't bet on it, scumbag,' Jake retorted. 'You're getting awful heavy.' The strain of supporting the Bringer's weight was indeed beginning to tell on his muscles. They were taut, shooting with pain.

'Drop me then,' Sicarius challenged. 'Let me fall. *Make* me fall.'

'I should do. You deserve to die.'

'Then kill me. Here, let me help you.' Sicarius shook and swung in Jake's grasp. 'Even harder to hold on now, isn't it?'

Jake braced himself as best he could. The agony stabbing at his arms and back and legs made him cry out. The darkness claimed the sound for its own.

'Kill me, Jake. Do it. The blessing of night is coming for us all, so what does it matter?'

'No!' Jake struggled to find his faith. He felt himself drawn nearer to the abyss, inch by inch. 'Takata will . . . stop you . . .'

'She will not. But let's say she does, *this time*.' Sicarius' laughter was hollow and mocking. The vortex whirled and writhed below. 'Next time she will fail. Because there'll *be* a next time if you let me live, Jake. And a next and a next. A hundred next times. A *thousand*.'

'Shut up.' Jake stared down into the terrorist's eyes and there was madness in them, and in his black stealth suit it seemed that Sicarius was a physical part of the seething, ferocious lunacy that filled the chasm, filled the world.

'Because I'll never stop, Jake. I'll go on killing, murdering, slaughtering —'

'Shut *up*!'

The darkness. The darkness was everywhere.

'The blessing of night I will bestow on all I meet.'

It was all he could see. It was all there was. Blackness entire. Blackness without reprieve. Blackness without redemption. Blackness without hope.

'I told you . . . I *told* you . . .' And his own voice was wild, crazy, and his senses were reeling as the night sea whirlpooled beneath him and he felt himself sliding and Sicarius was right and he had to be killed. By Jake. Now.

While the darkness inside him gave him strength.

His features contorted, possessed by something savage. 'Yes. *Yes!*' Sicarius sensed his triumph.

'No.'

A quieter voice, female. Like music in a morgue.

'No, Jake.'

'Dark?' As if he didn't know her. But she was suddenly there beside him and the green of her eyes was startling. 'I thought I told you . . . to wait for me.'

'I couldn't wait. You have to come back now, while you still can. Come back, Jake. Don't let Sicarius destroy you. Be who you were.'

'I'm not sure . . . I have the strength.'

'You do. We all do. You showed me that. It's make a choice time, Jake.'

He looked up at her dubiously. He couldn't hold on to Sicarius for much longer.

'If you kill Sicarius, he'll have won.' Those green eyes, large, pleading. It *wasn't* just blackness in the world.

And as he looked down at the founder of the Bringers of the Night, Jake's smile was as thin as the first ray of dawn.

Lori and Bex bolted from the elevator. No sign of anyone. Sicarius and Jake still had to be inside the crater. They darted for the ruined door.

'What if . . .?' Lori said, but got no further. Bex would understand her regardless. What if they were too late?

What if the other-dimensional energy had already erupted?

What if Jake had already killed Sicarius?

They emerged on to the platform.

'Jake! *Jake!*' And for a second Lori wanted to laugh, despite the manifest danger they still faced, laugh with relief because Jake was alive and so was Sicarius and the terrorist was being prodded from the bridge by Jake's shock blaster with his hands, one of them bleeding, on his head.

They were accompanied by an odd-looking girl who seemed to be keeping very close to Lori's ex-boyfriend.

Bex recognised the girl as Dark from the Deepwater One files. She didn't feel there was time to assess her relationship with Jake just now. Instead, 'Jake, come on! Run!' she screamed, gesturing wildly.

The walls of the crater shook. Bex felt she was in a spacecraft about to launch. The three on the bridge realised what was happening. They ran. Instinctively, even Sicarius, even while he shouted with deranged glee: 'You're too late! Night is upon us! Chaos has returned!'

'Shut,' barked Jake, '*up!*' But he glanced behind him just to see.

The inhibitors were blinking like eyes with grit in them. Had Takata failed? Was this the end? As great spouts of darkness geysered from the vortex, black spumes of fathomless, unbridled energy, powering upwards at incalculable speed.

Everyone was screaming. There was the groaning of metal pushed to the very limits of its resistance. Everyone was spilling into the corridor, on to the floor. A thunder unheard since the first day of creation boomed deafeningly in their ears.

Not even Jake dared look back now. It would be like staring into the soul of Death.

And then the power failed and they were cast into a lesser night themselves.

And they were cold. They were plunged into arctic deeps and the walls about them cracked like ice and they held each other for warmth, clasped each other close, Jake and Lori and Bex and Dark, and if they were going to die, they didn't want to be alone.

Sicarius, staggering to his feet. 'Take me, darkness. Bring me the blessing of your embrace. I am your servant Sicarius, Bringer of the Night.'

And then, as swiftly as it had begun, it was over. The cold began to ebb from their bones. Back-up systems revived the electricity. They could see each other again.

They were alive.

'No. It's not possible.' Somebody wasn't too happy about it.

'Takata?' said Jake.

Bex nodded. 'That was just the dimensional interface letting off some steam. You know how these things are.'

'But my darkness, my night, where are they?' Sicarius moaned. He stumbled back towards the tear in the wall, the crater beyond.

'Where do you think you're going, scumbag?' Jake cautioned.

'No, Jake. Let him see,' counselled Dark.

And Jake consented. And Lori and Bex stared at each other in bewilderment.

On the platform, Sicarius sank to his knees. 'You cheated me,' he wailed. 'I was so close, so close . . .'

'Them's the breaks,' Jake said, entirely without sympathy.

The particle inhibitors were fully operational again. Their steadfast light shone above the abyss. Beneath it, darkness flexed, reluctant, resentful, restrained. Order had been restored.

'Somehow, though,' anticipated Bex, 'I reckon this is one project that's going to be quietly put to rest.'

And above them, through the gaping hole where the escaping energies had shattered IDEA's roof, they could still see a stain of blackness swirling in the sky, but diminishing, dissolving with every second.

'Cut off from its source,' Jake theorised. 'Melting like a snowflake in summer. Kind of a discoloured snowflake, maybe, but you catch my drift.'

Lori's hand was on his. She was regarding him with gentle pride. 'You could have killed Sicarius but you didn't. I was worried. I thought . . .'

'So did I,' Jake said soberly. 'For a while there, so did I. But in the end, thanks to Dark' – he shot her a grateful glance – 'it struck me. You were right all along, Lo. How can you protect life if you don't value life? Even his.' Nodding towards Sicarius. 'Maybe I'm not cut out to be Jake Black after all. Maybe Black Ops aren't for me.' Jake gazed up again, in time to see the final wisps of darkness fade from the bright and shining sky. 'Let there be light,' he said.

'He's not coming back.'

Ten years ago, three children huddled on a luminous transitway, clinging to it as if it was a bridge keeping them safe from falling, and waited for the reappearance of a fourth.

The pale boy thought such a return increasingly unlikely. 'We've got to face facts, Jamie. Jake's lost.'

'No,' the girl said, scanning the awesome darkness like a lighthouse. 'I don't believe that.'

'You have to admit, though, Jamie,' the third member of the group, the boy with yellow hair, said, 'Lonny's got a point.'

'He'll be here.' The girl was certain. 'Jake won't let us down, Ford. You just have to trust him.'

'Yeah, after he left us in the dark,' complained Lonny. '*You* trust him if you want to. Me, I just want to go home.'

'Go on then, cry baby,' scolded Jamie. 'I'm not stopping you. Nobody's stopping you. But *I'm* waiting for Jake.'

'We won't go back without you, Jamie,' said Ford.

The girl's anxious face suddenly broke into a smile. 'You won't have to. Jake!'

Emerging from the ink. Stepping out of the darkness and on to the transitway. Untouched, it seemed. Untroubled. Grinning.

He was a short distance from them. 'Did you miss me?'

Jamie ran to him joyfully. Lonny and Ford kind of slouched.

'I knew you'd be all right!' the girl exclaimed. 'But what was it like?' She gazed into the night and shuddered. 'What was it like in *there*?'

'It makes you feel alone,' Jake said. 'For a moment it makes you feel like you're the only person in the world, but you just have to remember you're not. Then it's fine. There's nothing in the dark to really be afraid of.'

'That's great, Jake,' said Lonny, humouring him. 'Can we go home now?'

'Got a point,' said Ford.

'Sure,' said Jake. 'We can go home.'

But as they turned to place the glowing Dome before instead of behind them, he lingered to cast his gaze to dark and distant horizons.

'One day you'll leave us and you won't come back,' Jamie observed with quiet sadness. 'One day, Jake.'

He didn't deny it. 'Not for years yet, Jamie.'

The girl sighed. 'Guess that'll have to do.' She slipped her hand into his.

They began the long walk back to the Dome.

EPILOGUE

'I want to thank you, Jake,' said Dark.

'For what?'

'For *what*?'

She could have made a list. For not handing her over to the authorities with Sicarius, Dravic and the rest of the Bringers of the Night. For persuading Bex and that snooty Lori that she was a special case, that she deserved a second chance, that they owed her for standing with Jake when the chips were down. For supplying her with money, papers, the necessary mechanics to create and sustain a new identity and a new life.

For being with her as she commenced it.

She could have made a list, but she summarised. 'Oh, for everything.'

'My pleasure,' said Jake.

They seemed to be the only two people motionless in the whole station concourse. Everyone else was rushing *to* platforms, rushing *from* platforms, hectic and blinkered and swept along by the pace of their lives. The light trains were waiting, their solar sails impatient to unfurl.

'I guess I'd better . . .' The girl indicated the crowd. A small suitcase was by her feet.

'I guess so.' Jake squeezed her arms affectionately. He thought of the scars he'd seen before. He hoped they were healing. They had a good chance. In every other respect Dark seemed very different now from the damaged, defensive delinquent he'd first encountered in the mess hall of Deepwater One. It wasn't just her clothing, her appearance, though she seemed to have discovered a pride in both that hadn't been there before. It was more like something inside her that was finally being allowed expression, a confidence, a self-belief. It shone from her eyes. It made her, Jake thought, kind of beautiful. 'Goodbye, Dark,' he said.

'Sort of.' The girl smiled. 'Dark's already gone, Jake. I don't want to be her any more. I don't *have* to be her. That part of my life, it's dead and buried, and I've got a lot of making up for it to do. I haven't told you yet, but that false name you had your tech friend use in all my documentation? I got him to change it.'

'To what? Don't tell me. Jaketta. In my honour.'

'Sadly for you but luckily for me, no. I'm using my own name again. My *true* name.'

'I knew you had to have one.'

'You want to know what it is? You did back in Aquatraz.'

'Only if you want to tell me.' She did. She leaned forward and whispered the syllables into his ear. Jake pursed his lips and nodded sagely. 'I think I prefer Jaketta.'

'Oh, *you*.'

They laughed. It seemed natural. Then they kissed. That seemed natural too.

'Jake?' she said. 'I realise now what you meant that night in your room, why it would have been wrong for us to be together then. I understand. But if we ever see each other again, maybe we could, I don't know, try a different ending.'

'You'll find somebody,' said Jake. 'It's a big country.'

Several light trains pulled out of the station at once. The teenagers watched.

'Any idea where you're heading?' Jake asked.

'Forwards,' his companion said. 'But other than that, none at all. I'm gonna get on the first train I like the look of and go from there. *That* one.' She pointed. 'I like that one.' The randomness of her choice delighted her.

'You'd better run if you want to catch that one,' Jake warned.

'I will.' She picked up the suitcase. 'You'll wait though, won't you? Like you promised. You'll wait until the train's gone.'

'Even if I'm needed to save the world again.'

'And you'll remember me, won't you, Jake?' She gazed at him wistfully. 'I'll remember you.'

With that she was gone. And for a while Jake lost sight of her in the erratic crush of travellers. Then he saw her again, one final time, clambering aboard the train she'd selected to take her towards her future, and she was turning and waving and calling his name.

The doors were closing.

Jake waved back. He continued to wave as the light train departed, long after the girl could possibly have seen him. And long after that he simply stood there, silent, lost in thought.

Tomorrow he'd meet with Jonathan Deveraux.

Word had got around. Students darted out of classrooms to gawp at him as he strode the corridors of Spy High, like he was a celebrity or something. Like he'd returned from the dead. Jake tried to ignore them. They were first years, second years, still only kids. But he heard some of them gasp and some of them wow. He heard snippets of 'it's *true*' and 'the mind-wipe was a trick' and 'he took down Sicarius' and 'Daly's some dude'. He passed Mr Korita who acknowledged him as inscrutably as ever with a 'Jake.'

'Sir,' returned Jake. And took the elevator to Jonathan Deveraux's rooms.

It was like the scene of his recruitment into the Black Ops division, only in reverse. Jake stood within the circle of screens prepared for anything the founder of Spy High might decide, even a mind-wipe for real. He'd sooner have his secret agent career terminated than his newly restored belief in the sanctity of human life compromised. Was mind-wiping likely? Jonathan Deveraux made Mr Korita look positively extrovert.

'You wish to withdraw from covert counterterrorist operations,' said the computerised man. 'You wish to be returned to normal Deveraux assignments. You wish your conduct in the field to be governed again by this organisation's rules and regulations. You no longer wish to be Jake Black.'

'That's right, sir.'

Maybe there was a sigh from Deveraux, or maybe it was simply a hiss in the air-conditioning. 'How would you assess your mission, Agent Black?'

'I think it was a success, sir.'

'Despite your failure to achieve its ultimate objective? The terrorist known as Sicarius still lives.'

Jake defended himself. There was no point in doing anything else. Let the founder conclude whether he'd acted rightly or wrongly. 'But he's in custody, sir. He's helpless. And the Bringers of the Night have been smashed. I think . . . sir, I believe I acted in accordance with the Deveraux organisation's *primary* objective, to keep the world safe for tomorrow.'

'The world might be safer without Sicarius in it,' observed Jonathan Deveraux.

'With respect, though, sir,' ventured Jake, 'safer at what cost? What kind of world would it be if those committed to defending life resorted to killing as readily as those who despise it? In the end, wouldn't that have a detrimental effect on us? Over time, I mean. Wouldn't we risk losing sight of the value of life? Wouldn't we all be that little bit dehumanised?' Lori should be here, Jake thought. She'd be proud of him. 'I thought I could do it, sir, kill Sicarius, I mean. I wanted to, I really did. But at the last it was like, if I killed *him* I'd be killing part of *me* too. I don't know, I can't really explain it, but it would have been like a candle blowing out, a candle I couldn't have relit.'

Jake glanced up at one of Deveraux's faces. 'Am I making sense, sir?'

The founder said nothing for a long time, which suggested not. Then, 'The question of whether a society ever has the right to inflict death upon its enemies, whether by capital punishment or by the waging of war, has been debated for centuries,' Deveraux observed. 'It is one of Mankind's most insoluble moral dilemmas.' He considered further. 'An agent in the field cannot have his mind distracted by moral dilemmas. The mind of an agent in the field must be clear, alert and decisive, for an agent must be prepared at all times to act without question or compunction in the furtherance of his mission.'

And? Jake thought.

'It seems to have been a miscalculation on my part to place an agent in a situation where inherited moral scruples may come into conflict with mission objectives and thus potentially jeopardise the successful completion of an operation.' Jonathan Deveraux regarded Jake emotionlessly. 'Therefore, this organisation's covert counterterrorist programme will be discontinued. No disciplinary action will be taken against either you, Agent Daly, or against Agents Angel and Deveraux, whose involvement in this affair has also now come to my attention.'

'Sir?' Jake dared. 'You called me Agent Daly?'

'Indeed,' said Deveraux. 'You may return to your previous role, Agent Daly. Jake Black is no more.'

They were waiting for him in the rec room. Not only Lori and Bex, but Eddie, Cally and Ben as well, eager for news.

'I'm off the hook,' Jake announced.

Cheers. Whoops. (Both largely from Eddie.) Back-slapping. Hand-shaking.

'I'm pleased for you, Jake,' said Cally.

'I'm pleased for *us*,' crowed Eddie. 'At least we haven't got to track him down again. I've still got the lumps from last time.'

'Should have known it was too good to last,' Ben said slyly, but his handshake was strong. 'Welcome back, farm boy.'

'Hey, that's right,' Eddie remembered. 'Lori and Bex told us about Jake Mark II out in the fields. What's gonna happen to him?'

'We'll sort it out, Eddie, don't panic.' Jake brushed the issue aside. 'I just want to enjoy the moment for now, and I've got you two to thank for it.' He embraced Lori and Bex.

'You thank us by means of suffocation?' Bex complained playfully.

'And *we* didn't decide not to kill Sicarius, Jake,' Lori pointed out. 'You did. I'm so glad you're one of us again.'

'Obvious,' said Eddie. 'Inevitable. No one can keep Bond Team apart for long.'

'In some cases,' Ben muttered to Cally, 'more's the pity.'

'Did Dad say anything about Lo and me?' A trace of anxiety among the piercings.

'Did he?' Jake seemed to have forgotten. He stared into the distance absently. 'Um . . .'

'What?' Bex slapped his arm. 'Out of Black Ops and into psychological torture, is it?'

Jake grinned. 'Oh yeah, that was it. No disciplinary action will be taken.'

'Party *on*,' declared Bex.

'To coin a phrase from our Shakespeare study experiences,' added Lori, 'all's well that ends well.'

'You said it, Lo.'

But Jake wondered whether he ought to mention Jonathan Deveraux's bugging of their conversations. Decided against. Now probably wasn't the time – it'd certainly put a dampener on the mood. Besides, maybe Deveraux would think better of the practice anyway. Maybe eavesdropping on his students would go the same way as the Black Ops programme.

Jake sure hoped so.

Jonathan Deveraux was alone again. There was no apparent reason for his twelve heads to continue on screen, cold, austere faces, blank, impenetrable expressions, like the work of an alien artist who'd had a human being described to him but who'd never actually seen one.

Yet the heads remained, while complex machinery considered and calculated, while the computerised brain of Jonathan Deveraux worked, while evidence was weighed, conclusions drawn, plans determined.

Why? Perhaps because they served to remind the founder of Spy High of the man he'd once been. Perhaps because they enabled Deveraux to retain some last link with his human heritage.

Or perhaps not.

Because now, one by one, the twelve heads vanished,

and in their place there were only screens. In the rooms of Jonathan Deveraux, only screens and software and silence.

Nothing else was left.

About the Author

A. J. Butcher has been aware of the power of words since avoiding a playground beating aged seven because he 'told good stories'. He's been trying to do the same thing ever since. Writing serial stories at school that went on forever gave him a start (if not a finish). A degree in English Literature at Reading University kept him close to books, while a subsequent career as an advertising copywriter was intended to keep him creative. As it seemed to be doing a better job of keeping him inebriated, he finally became an English teacher instead. His influences include Dickens and Orwell, though Stan Lee, creator of the great Marvel super-heroes, is also an inspirational figure. In his spare time, A. J. reads too many comics, listens to too many '70s records and rants about politics to anyone who'll listen. When he was younger and fantasising about being a published author, he always imagined he'd invent a dashing, dynamic pseudonym for himself. Now that it's happened, however, he's sadly proven too vain for that. A. J. Butcher is his real and only name.

SPY HIGH
Series One

EPISODE ONE:

The Frankenstein Factory

ISBN 1904233139   £5.00

EPISODE TWO:

The Chaos Connection

ISBN 1904233147   £5.00

EPISODE THREE:

The Serpent Scenario

ISBN 1904233155   £5.00

EPISODE FOUR:

The Paranoia Plot

ISBN 1904233163   £5.00

EPISODE FIVE:

The Soul Stealer

ISBN 1904233171   £5.00

EPISODE SIX:

The Annihilation Agenda

ISBN 190423318X   £5.00

www.spyhigh.co.uk

www.atombooks.co.uk